MAN IN CONTROL

MAN IN CONTROL

DIANA PALMER

WHEELER
CHIVERS

This Large Print edition is published by Wheeler Publishing, Waterville, Maine, USA and by BBC Audiobooks Ltd, Bath, England.
Wheeler Publishing is an imprint of The Gale Group.
Wheeler is a trademark and used herein under license.
Copyright © 2003 by Diana Palmer.
The moral right of the author has been asserted.

LIBRARY OF CONGRESS CATALOGING-IN-PUBLICATION DATA

Palmer, Diana.
   Man in control / by Diana Palmer.
     p. cm. — (Wheeler Publishing large print romance)
   ISBN-13: 978-1-59722-648-6 (hardcover : alk. paper)
   ISBN-10: 1-59722-648-3 (hardcover : alk. paper)
   1. United States. Drug Enforcement Administration — Officials and employees — Fiction. 2. Undercover operations — Fiction. 3. Drug traffic — Fiction. 4. Texas — Fiction. 5. Large type books. I. Title.
PS3566.A513M35 2007
813'.54—dc22   2007033386

BRITISH LIBRARY CATALOGUING-IN-PUBLICATION DATA AVAILABLE

Published in 2007 in the U.S. by arrangement with Harlequin Books S.A.
Published in 2008 in the U.K. by arrangement with Harlequin Enterprises II B.V.

U.K. Hardcover: 978 1 405 64278 1 (Chivers Large Print)
U.K. Softcover: 978 1 405 64279 8 (Camden Large Print)

Printed in the United States of America on permanent paper
10 9 8 7 6 5 4 3 2 1

In loving memory of Diana Galloway

PROLOGUE

Alexander Tyrell Cobb glared at his desk in the Houston Drug Enforcement Administration office with barely contained frustration. There was a photograph of a lovely woman in a ball gown in an expensive frame, the only visible sign of any emotional connections. Like the conservative clothes he wore to work, the photograph gave away little of the private man.

The photograph was misleading. The woman in it wasn't a close friend. She was a casual date, when he was between assignments. The frame had been given to him with the photo in it. He'd never put a woman's photo in a frame. Well, except for Jodie Clayburn. She and his sister, Margie, were best friends from years past. Most of the family photos he had included Jodie. She wasn't really family, of course. But there was no other Cobb family left, just as there was no other Clayburn family left. The three survivors of the two families were a forced mixture of different lifestyles.

Jodie was in love with Alexander. He knew it, and tried not to acknowledge it. She was totally wrong for him. He had no desire to marry and have a family. On the other hand, if he'd been seriously interested in children and a home life, Jodie would have been at the top of his list of potential mates. She had wonderful qualities. He wasn't about to tell her so. She'd been hung up on him in the past to a disturbing degree. He'd managed to keep her at arm's length, and he had no plans to lessen the space between them. He was married to his job.

Jodie, on the other hand, was an employee at a local oil corporation which was being used in an international drug smuggling operation. Alexander was almost certain of it. But he couldn't prove it. He was going to have to find some way to investigate one of Jodie's acquaintances without letting anyone realize they were being watched.

In the meantime, there was a party planned at the Cobb ranch in Jacobsville, Texas, on Saturday. He dreaded it already. He hated parties. Margie had already invited Jodie, probably because their housekeeper, Jessie, refused to work that weekend. Jodie cooked with a masterful hand, and she could make canapés. Kirry had been invited, too, because Margie was a budding dress designer who needed a friend in the business. Kirry was senior buyer for the department store where she worked. She was pretty and capable, but Alexander found her good company and not much more. Their relationship had always been lukewarm and even now, it was slowly fizzling out. She was demanding. He had enough demands on the job.

He put the picture facedown on his desk and pulled a file folder closer, opening it to the photograph of a suspected drug smuggler who was working out of Houston. He had his work cut out for him. He wished he could avoid going home for the party, but Margie would never forgive him. If he didn't show up, neither would Kirry, and Alexander would never hear the end of it. He put the weekend to the back of his mind and concentrated on the job at hand.

ONE

There was no way out of it. Margie Cobb had invited her to a party on the family ranch in Jacobsville, Texas. Jodie Clayburn had gone through her entire repertoire of excuses. Her favorite was that, given the right incentive, Margie's big brother, Alexander Tyrell Cobb, would feed her to his cattle. Not even that one had worked.

"He hates me, Margie," she groaned over the phone from her apartment in Houston, Texas. "You know he does. He'd be perfectly happy if I stayed away from him for the rest of my natural life and he never had to see me again."

"That's not true," Margie defended. "Lex really likes you, I know he does," she added with forced conviction, using the nickname that only a handful of people on earth were allowed to use. Jodie wasn't one of them.

"Right. He just hides his affection for me in bouts of bad temper laced with sarcasm,"

11

came the dry reply.

"Sure," Margie replied with failing humor.

Jodie lay back on her sofa with the freedom phone at her ear and pushed back her long blond hair. It was getting too long. She really needed to have it cut, but she liked the feel of it. Her gray eyes smiled as she remembered how much Brody Vance liked long hair. He worked at the Ritter Oil Corporation branch office in Houston with her, and was on the management fast track. As Jody was. She was administrative assistant to Brody, and if Brody had his way, she'd take his job as Human Resources generalist when he moved up to Human Resources manager. He liked her. She liked him, too. Of course he had a knockout girlfriend who was a Marketing Division manager in Houston, but she was always on the road somewhere. He was lonely. So he had lunch frequently with Jodie. She was trying very hard to develop a crush on him. He was beginning to notice her. Alexander had accused her of trying to sleep her way to the executive washroom . . .

"I was not!" she exclaimed, remembering his unexpected visit to her office with an executive of the company who was a personal friend. It had played havoc with her nerves and her heart. Seeing Alexander unexpectedly melted her from the neck down, despite her best efforts not to let him affect her.

"Excuse me?" Margie replied, aghast.

Jodie sat up quickly. "Nothing!" she said. "Sorry. I was just thinking. Did you know that Alexander has a friend who works for my company?"

There was a long pause. "He does?"

"Jasper Duncan, the Human Resources manager for our division."

"Oh. Yes. Jasper!" There was another pause. "How do you know about that?"

"Because Mr. Duncan brought him right to my desk while I was talking to a . . . well, to a good friend of mine, my boss."

"Right, the one he thinks you're sleeping with."

"Margie!" she exploded.

There was an embarrassed laugh. "Sorry. I know there's nothing going on. Alexander always thinks the worst of people. You know about Rachel."

"Everybody knows about Rachel," she muttered. "It was six years ago and he still throws her up to us."

"We did introduce him," Margie said defensively.

"Well, how were we to know she was a female gigolo who was only interested in

13

marrying a rich man? She should have had better sense than to think Alexander would play that sort of game, anyway!"

"You do know him pretty well, don't you?" Margie murmured.

"We all grew up together in Jacobsville, Texas," Jodie reminded her. "Sort of," she added pensively. "Alexander was eight years ahead of us in school, and then he moved to Houston to work for the DEA when he got out of college."

"He's still eight years ahead of us," Margie chuckled. "Come on. You know you'll hate yourself if you miss this party. We're having a houseful of people. Derek will be there," she added sweetly, trying to inject a lure.

Derek was Margie's distant cousin, a dream of a man with some peculiar habits and a really weird sense of humor.

"You know what happened the last time Derek and I were together," Jodie said with a sense of foreboding.

"Oh, I'm sure Alexander has forgotten about *that* by now," she was assured.

"He has a long memory. And Derek can talk me into anything," Jodie added worriedly.

"I'll hang out with both of you and protect you from dangerous impulses. Come on.

Say yes. I've got an opportunity to show my designs. It depends on this party going smoothly. And I've made up this marvelous dress pattern I want to try out on you. For someone with the body of a clotheshorse, you have no sense of style at all!"

"You have enough for both of us. You're a budding fashion designer. I'm a lady executive. I have to dress the part."

"Baloney. When was the last time your boss wore a black dress to a party?"

Jodie was remembering a commercial she'd seen on television with men in black dresses. She howled, thinking of Alexander's hairy legs in a short skirt. Then she tried to imagine where he'd keep his sidearm in a short skirt, and she really howled.

She told Margie what she was thinking, and they both collapsed into laughter.

"Okay," she capitulated at last. "I'll come. But if I break a tree limb over your brother's thick skull, you can't say you weren't forewarned."

"I swear, I won't say a word."

"Then I'll see you Friday afternoon about four," Jodie said with resignation. "I'll rent a car and drive over."

"Uh, Jodie . . ."

She groaned. "All right, Margie, all right, I'll fly to the Jacobsville airport and you can pick me up there."

"Great!"

"Just because I had two little bitty fender benders," she muttered.

"You totaled two cars, Josie, and Alexander had to bail you out of jail after the last one . . ."

"Well, that stupid thickheaded barbarian deserved to be hit! He called me a . . . well, never mind, but he asked for a punch in the mouth!" Josie fumed.

Margie was trying not to laugh. Again.

"Anyway, it was only a small fine and the judge took my side when he heard the whole story," she said, ignoring Margie's quick reminder that Alexander had talked to the judge first. "Not that your brother ever let me forget it! Just because he works for the Justice Department is no reason for him to lecture me on law!"

"We just want you to arrive alive, darling," Margie drawled. "Now throw a few things into a suitcase, tell your boss you have a sick cousin you have to take care of before rush hour, and we'll . . . *I'll* . . . meet you at the airport Friday afternoon. You phone and tell me your flight number, okay?"

"Okay," Josie replied, missing the slip.

"See you then! We're going to have a ball."

"Sure we are," Josie told her. But when

she hung up, she was calling herself all sorts of names for being such a weakling. Alexander was going to cut her up, she just knew it. He didn't like her. He never had. He'd gotten more antagonistic since she moved to Houston, where he worked, too. Further, it would probably mean a lot of work for Jodie, because she usually had to prepare meals if she showed up. The family cook, Jessie, hated being around Alexander when he was home, so she ran for the hills. Margie couldn't cook at all, so Jodie usually ended up with KP. Not that she minded. It was just that she felt used from time to time.

And despite Margie's assurances, she knew she was in for the fight of her life once she set foot on the Cobb ranch. At least Margie hadn't said anything about inviting Alexander's sometimes-girlfriend, Kirry Dane. A weekend with the elegant buyer for an exclusive Houston department store would be too much.

The thing was, she had to go when Margie asked her. She owed the Cobbs so much. When her parents, small Jacobsville ranchers, had been drowned in a riptide during a modest Florida vacation at the beach, it had been Alexander who flew down to take care of all the arrangements and comfort a devastated seventeen-year-old Jodie. When she entered business college, Alexander had gone with her to register and paid the fees himself. She spent every holiday with Margie. Since the death of the Cobbs' father, and their inheritance of the Jacobsville ranch property, she'd spent her vacation every summer there with Margie. Her life was so intertwined with that of the Cobbs that she couldn't even imagine life without them.

But Alexander had a very ambiguous relationship with Jodie. From time to time he was affectionate, in his gruff way. But he also seemed to resent her presence and he picked at her constantly. He had for the past year.

She got up and went to pack, putting the antagonism to the back of her mind. It did no good to dwell on her confrontations with Alexander. He was like a force of nature which had to be accepted, since it couldn't be controlled.

The Jacobsville Airport was crowded for a Friday afternoon. It was a tiny airport compared to those in larger cities, but a lot of people in south Texas used it for commuter flights to San Antonio and Houston. There was a restaurant and two concourses, and the halls were lined with beautiful paintings of traditional Texas scenery.

Jodie almost bowed under the weight of her oversized handbag and the unruly carry-on bag whose wheels didn't quite work. She looked around for Margie. The brunette wouldn't be hard to spot because she was tall for a woman, and always wore something striking — usually one of her own flamboyant designs.

But she didn't see any tall brunettes. What she did see, and what stopped her dead in her tracks, was a tall and striking dark-haired man in a gray vested business suit. A man with broad shoulders and narrow hips and big feet in hand-tooled leather boots. He turned, looking around, and spotted her. Even at the distance, those deep-set, cold green eyes were formidable. So was he. He looked absolutely furious.

She stood very still, like a woman confronted with a spitting cobra, and waited while he approached her with the long, quick stride she remembered from years of painful confrontations. Her chin lifted and her eyes narrowed. She drew in a quick breath, and geared up for combat.

Alexander Tyrell Cobb was thirty-three. He was a senior agent for the Drug Enforcement Administration. Usually, he worked out of Houston, but he was on vacation for

19

a week. That meant he was at the family ranch in Jacobsville. He'd grown up there, with Margie, but their mother had taken them from their father after the divorce and had them live with her in Houston. It hadn't been until her death that they'd finally been allowed to return home to their father's ranch. The old man had loved them dearly. It had broken his heart when he'd lost them to their mother.

Alexander lived on the ranch sporadically even now, when he wasn't away on business. He also had an apartment in Houston. Margie lived at the ranch all the time, and kept things running smoothly while her big brother was out shutting down drug smugglers.

He looked like a man who could do that single-handed. He had big fists, like his big feet, and Jodie had seen him use them once on a man who slapped Margie. He rarely smiled. He had a temper like a scalded snake, and he was all business when he tucked that big .45 automatic into its hand-tooled leather holster and went out looking for trouble.

In the past two years, he'd been helping to shut down an international drug lord, Manuel Lopez, who'd died mysteriously in an explosion in the Bahamas. Now he was after the dead drug lord's latest successor, a Central American national who was reputed to have business connections in the port city of Houston.

She'd developed a feverish crush on him when she was in her teens. She'd written him a love poem. Alexander, with typical efficiency, had circled the grammatical and spelling errors and bought her a supplemental English book to help her correct the mistakes. Her self-esteem had taken a serious nosedive, and after that, she kept her deepest feelings carefully hidden.

She'd seen him only a few times since her move to Houston when she began attending business college. When she visited Margie these days, Alexander never seemed to be around except at Christmas. It was as if he'd been avoiding her. Then, just a couple of weeks ago, he'd dropped by her office to see Jasper. It had been a shock to see him unexpectedly, and her hands had trembled on her file folders, despite her best efforts to play it cool. She wanted to think she'd outgrown her flaming crush on him. Sadly, it had only gotten worse. It was easier on her nerves when she didn't have to see him. Fortunately it was a big city and they didn't travel in the same circles. But she didn't know where Alexander's office or apartment were, and she didn't ask.

In fact, her nerves were already on edge right now, just from the level, intent stare of those green eyes across a crowded concourse. She clutched the handle of her wheeled suitcase with a taut grip. Alexander made her knees weak.

He strode toward her. He never looked right or left. His gaze was right on her the whole way. She wondered if he was like that on the job, so intent on what he was doing that he seemed relentless.

He was a sexy beast, too. There was a tightly controlled sensuality in every movement of those long, powerful legs, in the way he carried himself. He was elegant, arrogant. Jodie couldn't remember a time in her life when she hadn't been fascinated by him. She hoped it didn't show. She worked hard at pretending to be his enemy.

He stopped in front of her and looked down his nose into her wide eyes. His were green, clear as water, with dark rims that made them seem even more piercing. He had thick black eyelashes and black eyebrows that were as black as his neatly cut, thick, straight hair.

"You're late," he said in his deep, gravelly voice, throwing down the gauntlet at once. He looked annoyed, half out of humor and wanting someone to bite.

"I can't fly the plane," she replied sarcastically. "I had to depend on *men* for that."

He gave her a speaking glance and turned. "The car's in the parking lot. Let's go."

"Margie was supposed to meet me," she muttered, dragging her case behind her.

"Margie knew I had to be here anyway, so she had me wait for you," he said enigmatically. "I never knew a woman who could keep an appointment, anyway."

The carry-on bag fell over for the tenth time. She muttered and finally just picked the heavy thing up. "You might offer to help me," she said, glowering at her companion.

His eyebrows arched. "Help a woman carry a heavy load? My God, I'd be stripped, lashed to a rail and carried through Houston by torchlight!"

She gave him a seething glance. "Manners don't go out of style!"

"Pity I never had any to begin with." He watched her struggle with the luggage, green eyes dancing with pure venom.

She was sweating already. "I hate you," she said through her teeth as she followed along with him.

"That's a change," he said with a shrug, pushing back his jacket as he dug into his slacks pocket for his car keys.

A security guard spotted the pistol on his belt and came forward menacingly. With meticulous patience, and very carefully, Alexander reached into the inside pocket of his suit coat and produced his badge and ID. He had it out before the guard reached them.

The man took it. "Wait a minute," he said, and moved aside to check it out over the radio.

"Maybe you're on a wanted list somewhere," Jodie said enthusiastically. "Maybe they'll put you in jail while they check out your ID!"

"If they do," he replied nonchalantly, "rent-a-cop over there will be looking for another job by morning."

He didn't smile as he said it, and Jodie knew he meant what he was saying. Alexander had a vindictive streak a mile wide. There was a saying among law enforcement people that Cobb would follow you all the way to hell to get you if you crossed him. From their years of uneasy acquaintance, she knew it was more than myth.

The security guard came back and handed Alexander his ID. "Sorry, sir, but it's my job to check out suspicious people."

Alexander glared at him. "Then why haven't you checked out the gentleman in the silk suit over there with the bulge in his hatband? He's terrified that you're going to notice him."

The security guard frowned and glanced toward the elegant man, who tugged at his collar. "Thanks for the tip," he murmured, and started toward the man.

"You might have offered to lend him your gun," she told Alexander.

"He's got one. Of a sort," he added with disgust at the pearl-handled sidearm the security guard was carrying.

"Men have to have their weapons, don't they?" she chided.

He gave her a quick glance. "With a mouth like yours, you don't need a weapon. Careful you don't cut your chin with that tongue."

She aimed a kick at his shin and missed, almost losing her balance.

"Assault on a law enforcement officer is a felony," he pointed out without even breaking stride.

She recovered her balance and went out the door after him without another word. If they ever suspended the rules for one day, she knew who she was going after!

Once they reached his car, an elegant white Jaguar S-type, he did put her bags in the trunk — but he left her to open her own door and get in. It wasn't surprising to find him driving such a car, on a federal agent's salary, because he and Margie were independently wealthy. Their late mother had left them both well-off, but unlike Margie, who loved the social life, Alexander refused to live on an inheritance. He enjoyed working for his living. It was one of many things Jodie admired about him.

The admiration didn't last long. He threw down the gauntlet again without hesitation. "How's your boyfriend?" he asked as he pulled out into traffic.

"I don't have a boyfriend!" she snapped, still wiping away sweat. It was hot for August, even in south Texas.

"No? You'd like to have one, though, wouldn't you?" He adjusted the rearview mirror as he stopped at a traffic light.

"He's my boss. That's all."

"Pity. You could hardly take your eyes off him, that day I stopped by your office."

"*He's* handsome," she said with deliberate emphasis.

His eyebrow jerked. "Looks don't get you promoted in the Drug Enforcement Administration," he told her.

"You'd know. You've worked for it half your life."

"Not quite half. I'm only thirty-three."

"One foot in the grave . . ."

He glanced at her. "You're twenty-five, I believe? And never been engaged?"

He knew that would hurt. She averted her gaze to the window. Until a few months ago, she'd been about fifty pounds overweight and not very careful about her clothing or makeup. She was still clueless about how to dress. She dressed like an overweight woman, with loose clothing that showed nothing of her pretty figure. She folded her arms over her breasts defensively.

"I can't go through with this," she said through her teeth. "Three days of you will put me in therapy!"

He actually smiled. "That would be worth putting up with three days of you to see."

She crossed her legs under her full skirt and concentrated on the road. Her eyes caressed the silky brown bird's-eye maple that graced the car's dash and steering wheel.

"Margie promised she'd meet me," she muttered, repeating herself.

"She told me you'd be thrilled if I did," he replied with a searing glance. "You're still hung up on me, aren't you?" he asked with faint sarcasm.

Her jaw fell. "She lied! I did not say I'd

be thrilled for you to meet me!" she raged. "I only came because she promised that she'd be here when I landed. I wanted to rent a car and drive!"

His green eyes narrowed on her flushed face. "That would have been suicide," he murmured. "Or homicide, depending on your point of view."

"I can drive!"

"You and the demolition derby guys," he agreed. He accelerated around a slow-moving car and the powerful Jaguar growled like the big cat it was named for. She glanced at him and saw the pure joy of the car's performance in his face as he slid effortlessly back into the lane ahead of the slow car. He enjoyed fast cars and, gossip said, faster women. But that side of his life had always been concealed from Jodie. It was as if he'd placed her permanently off-limits and planned to keep her there.

"At least I don't humiliate other drivers by streaking past them at jet fighter speed!" she raged. She was all but babbling, and after only ten minutes of his company. Seething inwardly, she turned toward the window so that she wouldn't have to look at him.

"I wasn't streaking. I'm doing the speed limit," he said. He glanced at the speedometer, smiled faintly and eased up on the accelerator. His eyes slid over Jodie curiously. "You've lost so much weight, I hardly recognized you when I stopped by to talk to Jasper."

"Right. I looked different when I was fat."

"You were never fat," he shot back angrily. "You were voluptuous. There's a difference."

She glanced at him. "I was terribly overweight."

"And you think men like to run their hands over bones, do you?"

She shifted in her seat. "I wouldn't know."

"You had a low self-image. You still have it. There's nothing wrong with you. Except for that sharp tongue," he added.

"Look who's complaining!"

"If I don't yell, nobody listens."

"You never yell," she corrected. "You can look at people and make them run for cover."

He smiled without malice. "I practice in my bathroom mirror."

She couldn't believe she'd heard that.

"You need to start thinking about a Halloween costume," he murmured as he made a turn.

"For what? Are you going to hire me out for parties?" she muttered.

29

"For our annual Halloween party next month," he said with muted disgust. "Margie's invited half of Jacobsville to come over in silly clothes and masks to eat candy apples."

"What are you coming as?"

He gave her a careless glance. "A Drug Enforcement Agency field agent."

She rolled her eyes toward the ceiling of the car.

"I make a convincing DEA field agent," he persisted.

"I wouldn't argue with that," she had to agree. "I hear that Manuel Lopez mysteriously blew up in the Bahamas the year before last, and nobody's replaced him yet," she added. "Did you have anything to do with his sudden demise?"

"DEA agents don't blow up drug lords. Not even one as bad as Lopez."

"Somebody did."

He glanced at her with a faint smile. "In a manner of speaking."

"One of the former mercs from Jacobsville, I heard."

"Micah Steele was somewhere around when it happened. He's never been actually connected with Lopez's death."

"He moved back here and married Callie

30

Kirby, didn't he? They have a little girl now."

He nodded. "He's practicing medicine at Jacobsville General as a resident, hoping to go into private practice when he finishes his last semester of study."

"Lucky Callie," she murmured absently, staring out the window. "She always wanted to get married and have kids, and she was crazy about Micah most of her life."

He watched her curiously. "Didn't you want to get married, too?"

She didn't answer. "So now that Lopez is out of the way, and nobody's replaced him, you don't have a lot to do, do you?"

He laughed shortly. "Lopez has a new successor, a Peruvian national living in Mexico on an open-ended visa. He's got colleagues in Houston helping him smuggle his product into the United States."

"Do you know who they are?" she asked excitedly.

He gave her a cold glare. "Oh, sure, I'm going to tell you their names right now."

"You don't have to be sarcastic, Cobb," she said icily.

One thick eyebrow jerked. "You're the only person I know, outside work, who uses my last name as if it were my first name."

"You don't use my real name, either."

31

"Don't I?" He seemed surprised. He glanced at her. "You don't look like a Jordana."

"I never thought I looked like a Jordana, either," she said with a sigh. "My mother loved odd names. She even gave them to the cats."

Remembering her mother made her sad. She'd lost both parents in a freak accident during a modest vacation in Florida after her high school graduation. Her parents had gone swimming in the ocean, having no idea that the pretty red flags on the beach warned of treacherous riptides that could drown even experienced swimmers. Which her mother and father were not. She could still remember the horror of it. Alexander had come to take care of the details, and to get her back home. Odd how many tragedies and crises he'd seen her through over the years.

"Your mother was a sweet woman," he recalled. "I'm sorry you lost her. And your father."

"He was a sweet man, too," she recalled. It had been eight years ago, and she could remember happy times now, but it still made her sad to think of them.

"Strange, isn't it, that you don't take after either of them?" he asked caustically. "No man in his right mind could call you 'sweet.' "

"Stop right there, Cobb," she threatened, using his last name again. It was much more comfortable than getting personal with the nickname Margie used for him. "I could say things about you, too."

"What? That I'm dashing and intelligent and the answer to a maiden's prayer?" He pursed his lips and glanced her way as he pulled into the road that led to the ranch. "Which brings up another question. Are you sleeping with that airheaded boss of yours at work yet?"

"He is not airheaded!" she exclaimed, offended.

"He eats tofu and quiche, he drives a red convertible of uncertain age, he plays tennis and he doesn't know how to program a computer without crashing the system."

That was far too knowledgeable to have come from a dossier. Her eyes narrowed. "You've had him checked out!" she accused with certainty.

He only smiled. It wasn't a nice smile.

Two

"You can't go around snooping into people's private lives like that," Jodie exclaimed heatedly. "It's not right!"

"I'm looking for a high-level divisional manager who works for the new drug lord in his Houston territory," he replied calmly. "I check out everybody who might have an inkling of what's going on." He turned his head slightly. "I even checked you out."

"Me?" she exclaimed.

He gave her a speaking look. "I should have known better. If I had a social life like yours, I'd join a convent."

"I can see you now, in long skirts . . ."

"It was a figure of speech," he said curtly. He pulled into the road that led up to the ranch house. "You haven't been on a date in two years. Amazing, considering how many eligible bachelors there are in your building alone, much less the whole of Houston." He gave her a penetrating stare.

"Are you sure you aren't still stuck on me?"

She drew in a short breath. "Oh, sure, I am," she muttered. "I only come down here so that I can sit and moon over you and think of ways to poison all your girlfriends."

He chuckled in spite of himself. "Okay. I get the idea."

"Who in my building do you suspect, exactly?" she persisted.

He hesitated. His dark brows drew together in a frown as the ranch house came into view down the long, dusty road. "I can't tell you that," he said. "Right now it's only a suspicion."

"I could help you trap him," she volunteered. "If I get a gun, that is. I won't help you if I have to be unarmed."

He chuckled again. "You shoot like you drive, Jodie."

She made an angry sound in her throat. "I could shoot just fine if I got enough practice. Is it my fault that my landlord doesn't like us busting targets in my apartment building?"

"Have Margie invite you down just to shoot. She can teach you as well as I can."

It was an unpleasant reminder that he wasn't keen on being with her.

"I don't remember asking you to teach me anything," she returned.

He pulled up in front of the house. "Well, not lately, at least," he had to agree.

Margie heard the car drive up and came barreling out onto the porch. She was tall, like Alexander, and she had green eyes, too, but her dark hair had faint undertones of auburn. She was pretty, unlike poor Jodie, and she wore anything with flair. She designed and made her own clothes, and they were beautiful.

She ran to Jodie and hugged her, laughing. "I'm so glad you came!"

"I thought you were going to pick me up at the airport, Margie," came the droll reply.

Margie looked blank for an instant. "Oh, gosh, I was, wasn't I? I got busy with a design and just lost all track of time. Besides, Lex had already gone to the airport to pick up Kirry, but she couldn't get his cell phone, so she phoned me and said she was delayed until tomorrow afternoon. He was right there already, so I just phoned him and had him bring you home."

Kirry was Alexander's current girlfriend. The fashion buyer had just returned home recently from a buying trip to Paris. It didn't occur to Margie that it would have been pure torture to have to ride to the ranch with Alexander and his girlfriend. But, then, Margie didn't think things through. And to give her credit, she didn't realize that Jodie was still crazy about Alexander Cobb.

"She's coming down tomorrow to look at some of my new designs," Margie continued, unabashed, "and, of course, for the party in her honor that we're giving here. She leads a very busy life."

Jodie felt her heart crashing at her feet, and she didn't dare show it. A weekend with Kirry Dane drooling over Alexander, and vice versa. Why hadn't she argued harder and stayed home?

Alexander checked his watch. "I've got to make a few phone calls, then I'm going to drive into town and see about that fencing I ordered."

"That's what we have a foreman for," Margie informed him.

"Chayce went home to Georgia for the weekend. His father's in the hospital."

"You didn't tell me that!"

"Did you need to know?" he shot right back.

Margie shook her head, exasperated, as he just walked away without a backward glance. "I do live here, too," she muttered, but it was too late. He'd already gone into the house.

"I'm going to be in the way if the party's for Kirry," Jodie said worriedly. "Honestly,

Margie, you shouldn't have invited me. No wonder Alexander's so angry!"

"It's my house, too, and I can invite who I like," Margie replied curtly, intimating that she and Alexander had argued about Jodie's inclusion at the party. That hurt even more. "You're my best friend, Jodie, and I need an ego boost," Margie continued unabashed. "Kirry is so worldly and sophisticated. She hates it here and she makes me feel insecure. But I need her help to get my designs shown at the store where she works. So, you're my security blanket." She linked her arm with Jodie's. "Besides, Kirry and Lex together get on my nerves."

What about my nerves? Jodie was wondering. And my heart, having to see Alexander with Kirry all weekend? But she only smiled and pretended that it didn't matter. She was Margie's friend, and she owed her a lot. Even if it was going to mean eating her heart out watching the man she loved hang on to that beautiful woman, Kirry Dane.

Margie stopped just before they went into the house. She looked worried. "You have gotten over that crush you had on my brother . . . ?" she asked quickly.

"You and your brother!" Jodie gasped. "Honestly, I'm too old for schoolgirl crushes," she lied through her teeth, "and besides, there's this wonderful guy at the office that I like a lot. It's just that he's going with someone."

Margie grimaced. "You poor kid. It's always like that with you, isn't it?"

"Go right ahead and step on my ego, don't mind me," Jodie retorted.

Margie flushed. "I'm a pig," she said. "Sorry, Jodie. I don't know what's the matter with me. Yes, I do," she added at once. "Cousin Derek arrived unexpectedly this morning. Jessie's already threatened to cook him up with a pan of eggs, and one of the cowboys ran a tractor through a fence trying to get away from him. In fact, Jessie remembered that she could have a weekend off whenever she wanted, so she's gone to Dallas for the weekend to see her brother. And here I am with no cook and a party tomorrow night!"

"Except me?" Jodie ventured, and her heart sank again when she saw Margie's face. No wonder she'd been insistent. There wouldn't be any food without someone to cook it, and Margie couldn't cook.

"You don't mind, do you, dear?" Margie asked quickly. "After all, you do make the most scrumptious little canapés, and you're a great cook. Even Jessie asks you for recipes."

"No," Jodie lied. "I don't mind."

"And you can help me keep Derek out of Alexander's way."

"Derek." Jodie's eyes lit up. She loved the Cobbs' renegade cousin from Oklahoma. He was a rodeo cowboy who won belts at every competition, six foot two of pure lithe muscle, with a handsome face and a modest demeanor — when he wasn't up to some horrible devilment. He drove housekeepers and cowboys crazy with his antics, and Alexander barely tolerated him. He was Margie's favorite of their few cousins. Not that he was really a cousin. He was only related by marriage. Of course, Margie didn't know that. Derek had told Jodie once, but asked her not to tell. She wondered why.

"Don't even think about helping him do anything crazy while you're here," Margie cautioned. "Lex doesn't know he's here yet. I, uh, haven't told him."

"Margie!" came a thunderous roar from the general direction of Alexander's office.

Margie groaned. "Oh, dear, Lex does seem to know about Derek."

"My suitcase," Jodie said, halting, hoping to get out of the line of fire in time.

"Lex will bring it in, dear, come along." She almost dragged her best friend into the house.

Derek was leaning against the staircase banister, handsome as a devil, with dancing brown eyes and a lean, good-looking face under jet-black hair. In front of him, Alexander was holding up a rubber chicken by the neck.

"I thought you liked chicken," Derek drawled.

"Cooked," Alexander replied tersely. "Not in my desk chair pretending to be a cushion!"

"You could cook that, but the fumes would clear out the kitchen for sure," Derek chuckled.

Cobb threw it at the man, turned, went back into his office and slammed the door. Muttered curses came right through two inches of solid mahogany.

"Derek, how could you?" Margie wailed.

He tossed her the chicken and came forward to lift her up and kiss her saucily on the nose. "Now, now, you can't expect me to be dignified. It isn't in my nature. Hi, sprout!" he added, putting Margie down only to pick up Jodie and swing her around in a bear hug. "How's my best girl?"

"I'm just fine, Derek," she replied, kissing his cheek. "You look great."

"So do you." He let her dangle from his hands and his keen dark eyes scanned her flushed face. "Has Cobb been picking on you all the way home?" he asked lazily.

"Why can't you two call him Lex, like I do?" Margie wanted to know.

"He doesn't look like a Lex," Derek replied.

"He always picks on me," Jodie said heavily as Derek let her slide back onto her feet. "If he had a list of people he doesn't like, I'd lead it."

"We'd tie for that spot, I reckon," Derek replied. He gave Margie a slow, steady appraisal. "New duds? I like that skirt."

Margie grinned up at him. "I made it."

"Good for you. When are you going to have a show of all those pretty things you make?"

"That's what I'm working on. Lex's girlfriend Kirry is trying to get her store to let me do a parade of my designs."

"Kirry." Derek wrinkled his straight nose. "Talk about slow poison. And he thought Rachel was bad!"

"Don't mention Rachel!" Margie cautioned quickly.

"Kirry makes her look like a church mouse," Derek said flatly. "She's a social climber with dollar signs for eyes. Mark my words, it isn't his body she's after."

"He likes her," Margie replied.

"He likes liver and onions, too," Derek said, and made a horrible face.

Jodie laughed at the byplay.

Derek glanced at her. "Why doesn't he ever look at you, sprout? You'd be perfect for him."

"Don't be silly," Jodie said with a forced smile. "I'm not his type at all."

"You're not mercenary. You're a sucker for anyone in trouble. You like cats and dogs and children, and you don't like night life. You're perfect."

"He likes opera and theater," she returned.

"And you don't?" Derek asked.

Margie grabbed him by the arm. "Come on and let's have coffee while you tell us about your latest rodeo triumph."

"How do you know it was?" he teased.

"When have you ever lost a belt?" she replied with a grin.

Jodie followed along behind them, already uneasy about the weekend. She had a feeling that it wasn't going to be the best one of her life.

Later, Jodie escaped from the banter between Margie and her cousin and went out to the corral near the barn to look at the new calves. One of the older ranch hands, Johnny, came out to join her. He was missing a tooth in front from a bull's hooves and a finger from a too-tight rope that slipped. His chaps and hat and boots were worn and dirty from hard work. But he had a heart of pure gold, and Jodie loved him. He reminded her of her late father.

"Hey, Johnny!" she greeted, standing on the top rung of the wooden fence in old jeans, boots, and a long-sleeved blue checked shirt. Her hair was up in a ponytail. She looked about twelve.

He grinned back. "Hey, Jodie! Come to see my babies?"

"Sure have!"

"Ain't they purty?" he drawled, joining her at the fence, where she was feeding her eyes on the pretty little white-faced, red-coated calves.

"Yes, they are," she agreed with a sigh. "I miss this up in Houston. The closest I get to cattle is the rodeo when it comes to town."

He winced. "You poor kid," he said. "You lost everything at once, all them years ago."

That was true. She'd lost her parents and her home, all at once. If Alexander hadn't gotten her into business college, where she could live on campus, she'd have been homeless.

She smiled down at him. "Time heals even

the worst wounds, Johnny. Besides, I still get to come down here and visit once in a while."

He looked irritated. "Wish you came more than that Dane woman," he said under his breath. "Can't stand cattle and dust, don't like cowboys, looks at us like we'd get her dirty just by speaking to her."

She reached over and patted him gently on the shoulder. "We all have our burdens to bear."

He sighed. "I reckon so. Why don't you move back down here?" he added. "Plenty of jobs going in Jacobsville right now. I hear tell the police chief needs a new secretary."

She chuckled. "I'm not going to work for Cash Grier," she assured him. "They said his last secretary emptied the trash can over his head, and it was full of half-empty coffee cups and coffee grounds."

"Well, some folks don't take to police work," he said, but he chuckled.

"Nothing to do, Johnny?" came a deep, terse voice from behind Jodie.

Johnny straightened immediately. "Just started mucking out the stable, boss. I only came over to say howdy to Miss Jodie."

"Good to see you again, Johnny," she said.

"Same here, miss."

He tipped his hat and went slowly back

into the barn.

"Don't divert the hired help," Alexander said curtly.

She got down from the fence. It was a long way up to his eyes in her flat shoes. "He was a friend of my father's," she reminded him. "I was being polite."

She turned and started back into the house.

"Running away?"

She stopped and faced him. "I'm not going to be your whipping boy," she said.

His eyebrows arched. "Wrong gender."

"You know what I mean. You're furious that Derek's here, and Kirry's not, and you want somebody to take it out on."

He moved restlessly at the accusation. His scowl was suddenly darker. "Don't do that."

She knew what he meant. She could always see through his bad temper to the reason for it, something his own sister had never been able to do.

"Derek will leave in the morning and Kirry will be here by afternoon," she said. "Derek can't do that much damage in a night. Besides, you know how close he and Margie are."

"He's too flighty for her, distant relation or not," he muttered.

She sighed, looking up at him with quiet,

soft eyes full of memories. "Like me," she said under her breath.

He frowned. "What?"

"That's always been your main argument against me — that I'm too flighty. That's why you didn't like it when Derek was trying to get me to go out with him three years ago," she reminded him.

He stared at her for a few seconds, still scowling. "Did I say that?"

She nodded then turned away. "I've got to go help Margie organize the food and drinks," she added. "Left to her own devices, we'll be eating turkey and bacon roll-ups and drinking spring water."

"What did you have in mind?" he asked amusedly.

"A nice baked chicken with garlic-and-chives mashed potatoes, fruit salad, homemade rolls and biscuits, gravy, fresh asparagus, and a chocolate pound cake for dessert," she said absently.

"You can cook?" he asked, astonished.

She glared at him over one shoulder. "You didn't notice? Margie hasn't cooked a meal any time I've been down here for the weekend, except for one barbecue that the cowboys roasted a side of beef for."

He didn't say another word, but he looked unusually thoughtful.

The meal came out beautifully. By the time she had it on the table, Jodie was flushed from the heat of the kitchen and her hair was disheveled, but she'd produced a perfect meal.

Margie enthused over the results with every dish she tasted, and so did Derek. Alexander was unusually quiet. He finished his chocolate pound cake and a second cup of coffee before he gave his sister a dark look.

"You told me you'd been doing all the cooking when Jessie wasn't here and Jodie was," he said flatly.

Margie actually flushed. She dropped her fork and couldn't meet Jodie's surprised glance.

"You always made such a fuss of extra company when Jessie was gone," she protested without realizing she was only making things worse.

Alexander's teeth ground together when he saw the look on Jodie's face. He threw down his napkin and got noisily to his feet. "You're as insensitive as a cactus plant, Margie," he said angrily.

"You're better?" she retorted, with her

eyebrows reaching for her hairline. "You're the one who always complains when I invite Jodie, even though she hasn't got any family except us . . . oh, dear."

Jodie had already gotten to her own feet and was collecting dirty dishes. She didn't respond to the bickering. She felt it, though. It hurt to know that Alexander barely tolerated her; almost as much as it hurt to know Margie had taken credit for her cooking all these years.

"I'll help you clear, darlin'," Derek offered with a meaningful look at the Cobbs. "Both of you could use some sensitivity training. You just step all over Jodie's feelings without the least notice. Some 'second family' you turned out to be!"

He propelled Jodie ahead of him into the kitchen and closed the door. For once, he looked angry.

She smiled at him. "Don't take it so personally, Derek," she said. "Insults just bounce off me. I'm so used to Alexander by now that I hardly listen."

He tilted her chin up and read the pain in her soft eyes. "He walks on your heart every time he speaks to you," he said bluntly. "He doesn't even know how you feel, when a blind man could see it."

She patted his cheek. "You're a nice man, Derek."

He shrugged. "I've always been a nice man, for all the good it does me. Women flock to hang all over Cobb while he glowers and insults them."

"Someday a nice, sweet woman will come along and take you in hand, and thank God every day for you," she told him.

He chuckled. "Want to take me on?"

She wrinkled her nose at him. "You're very sweet, but I've got my eye on a rather nice man at my office. He's sweet, too, and his girlfriend treats him like dirt. He deserves someone better."

"He'd be lucky to get you," Derek said.

She smiled.

They were frozen in that affectionate tableau when the door opened and Alexander exploded into the room. He stopped short, obviously unsettled by what he thought he was seeing. Especially when Jodie jerked her hand down from Derek's cheek, and he let go of her chin.

"Something you forgot to say about Jodie's unwanted presence in your life?" Derek drawled, and for an instant, the smiling, gentle man Jodie knew became a threatening presence.

Alexander scowled. "Margie didn't mean

that the way it sounded," he returned.

"Margie never means things the way they sound," Derek said coldly, "but she never stops to think how much words can hurt, either. She walks around in a perpetual Margie-haze of self-absorption. Even now, Jodie's only here because she can make canapés for the party tomorrow night — or didn't you know?" he added with absolute venom.

Margie came into the room behind her brother, downcast and quiet. She winced as she met Derek's accusing eyes.

"I'm a pig," she confessed. "I really don't mean to hurt people. I love Jodie. She knows it, even if you don't."

"You have a great way of showing it, honey," Derek replied, a little less antagonistic to her than to her brother. "Inviting Jodie down just to cook for a party is pretty thoughtless."

Margie's eyes fell. "You can go home if you want to, Jodie, and I'm really sorry," she offered.

"Oh, for heaven's sake, I don't mind cooking!" Jodie went to Margie and hugged her hard. "I could always say no if I didn't want to do it! Derek's just being kind, that's all."

Margie glared at her cousin. "Kind."

Derek glared back. "Sure I am. It runs in

the family. Glad you could come, Jodie, want to wash and wax my car when you finish doing the dishes?" he added sarcastically.

"You stop that!" Margie raged at him.

"Then get in here and help her do the dishes," Derek drawled. "Or do your hands melt in hot water?"

"We do have a dishwasher," Alexander said tersely.

"Gosh! You've actually seen it, then?" Derek exclaimed.

Alexander said a nasty word and stormed out of the kitchen.

"One down," Derek said with twinkling eyes and looking at Margie. "One to go."

"Quit that, or she'll toss you out and I'll be stuck here with them and Kirry all weekend," Jodie said softly.

"Kirry?" He gaped at Margie. "You invited Kirry?"

Margie ground her teeth together and clenched her small hands. "She's the guest of honor!"

"Lord, give me a bus ticket!" He moved toward the door. "Sorry, honey, I'm not into masochism, and a night of unadulterated Kirry would put me in a mental ward. I'm leaving."

"But you just got here!" Margie wailed.

He turned at the door. "You should have told me who was coming to the party. I'd still be in San Antonio. Want to come with me, Jodie?" he offered. "I'll take you to a fiesta!"

Margie looked murderous. "She's my friend."

"She's not, or you wouldn't have forced her down here to suffer Kirry all weekend," he added.

"Give me a minute to get out of the line of fire, will you?" Jodie held up her hands and went back to the dining room to scoop up dirty dishes, forcibly smiling.

Derek glanced at the closed door, and moved closer to Margie. "Don't try to convince me that you don't know how Jodie feels about your brother."

"She got over that old crush years ago, she said so!" Margie returned.

"She lied," he said shortly. "She's as much in love with him as she ever was, not that either of you ever notice! It's killing her just to be around him, and you stick her with Kirry. How do you think she's going to feel, watching Kirry slither all over Cobb for a whole night?"

Margie bit her lower lip and looked hunted. "She said . . ."

"Oh, sure, she's going to tell you that she's

in love with Cobb." He nodded. "Great instincts, Marge."

"Don't call me Marge!"

He bent and brushed an insolent kiss across her parted lips, making her gasp. His dark eyes narrowed as he assayed the unwilling response. "Never thought of me like that, either, huh?" he drawled.

"You're . . . my . . . cousin," she choked.

"I'm no close relation to you at all, despite Cobb's antagonism. One day I'm going to walk out the door with you over my shoulder, and Cobb can do his worst." He winked at her. "See you, sweetheart."

He turned and ambled out the door. Margie was still staring after him helplessly and holding her hand to her lips when Jodie came in with another stack of dishes.

"What's wrong with you?" Jodie asked.

"Derek kissed me," she said in a husky tone.

"He's always kissing you."

Margie swallowed hard. "Not like this."

Jodie's eyebrows went up and she grinned. "I thought it was about time."

"What?"

"Nothing," Jodie said at once. "Here, can you open the dishwasher for me? My hands are full."

Margie broke out of her trance and went

to help, shell-shocked and quiet.

"Don't let Derek upset you," Jodie said gently. "He thinks he's doing me a favor, but he's not. I don't mind helping out, in any way I can. I owe you and Cobb so much . . ."

"You don't owe us a thing," Margie said at once. "Oh, Jodie, you shouldn't let me make use of you like this. You should speak up for yourself. You don't do that enough."

"I know. It's why I haven't advanced in the company," she had to admit. "I just don't like confrontations."

"You had enough of them as a kid, didn't you?" Margie asked.

Jodie flushed. "I loved my parents. I really did."

"But they fought, too. Just like ours. Our mother hated our father, even after he was dead. She drank and drank, trying to forget him, just the same. She soured my brother on women, you know. She picked on him from the time he was six, and every year it got worse. He had a roaring inferiority complex when he was in high school."

"Yes? Well, he's obviously got over it now," Jodie said waspishly.

Margie shook her head. "Not really. If he had, he'd know he could do better than Kirry."

"I thought you liked her!"

Margie looked shamefaced. "I do, sort of. Well, she's got an important job and she could really help me get my foot in the door at Weston's, the exclusive department store where she works."

"Oh, Margie," Jodie said wearily, shaking her head.

"I use people," Margie admitted. "But," she added brightly, "I try to do it in a nice way, and I always send flowers or presents or something afterward, don't I?"

Jodie laughed helplessly. "Yes, you do," she admitted. "Here, help me load up the dishes, and then you can tell me what sort of canapés you want me to make for tomorrow."

She didn't add that she knew she'd spend the whole day tomorrow making them, because the party was for almost forty people, and lunch had to be provided as well. It was a logistical nightmare. But she could cope. She'd done it before. And Margie was her best friend.

THREE

Jodie was up at dawn making biscuits and dough for the canapés. She'd only just taken up breakfast when Alexander came into the kitchen, wearing jeans and boots and a long-sleeved chambray shirt. He looked freshly showered and clean-shaven, his dark hair still damp.

"I've got breakfast," Jodie offered without looking too closely at him. He was overpowering in tight jeans and a shirt unbuttoned to his collarbone, where thick curling black hair peeked out. She had to fight not to throw herself at him.

"Coffee?" he murmured.

"In the pot."

He poured himself a cup, watching the deft motions of her hands as she buttered biscuits and scooped eggs onto a platter already brimming over with bacon and sausages.

"Aren't you eating?" he asked as he seated

57

himself at the table.

"Haven't time," she said, arranging a layer of canapés on a baking sheet. "Most of your guests are coming in time for lunch, so these have to be done now, before I get too busy."

His sensuous lips made a thin line. "I can't stand him, but Derek is right about one thing. You do let Margie use you."

"You and Margie were there when I had nobody else," she said without seeing the flinch of his eyelids. "I consider that she's entitled to anything I can ever do for her."

"You sell yourself short."

"I appreciate it when people do things for me without being asked," she replied. She put the canapés in the oven and set the timer, pushing back sweaty hair that had escaped from her bun.

His eyes went over her figure in baggy pants and an oversize T-shirt. "You dress like a bag lady," he muttered.

She glanced at him, surprised. "I dress very nicely at work."

"Like a dowager bag lady," he corrected. "You wear the same sort of clothes you favored when you were overweight. You're not anymore. Why don't you wear things that fit?"

It was surprising that he noticed her enough to even know what she was wearing. "Margie's the fashion model, not me," she reminded him. "Besides, I'm not the type for trendy stuff. I'm just ordinary."

He frowned. She had a real ego problem. He and Margie hadn't done much for it, either. She accepted anything that was thrown at her, as if she deserved it. He was surprised how much it bothered him, to see her so undervalued even by herself. Not that he was interested in her, he added silently. She wasn't his type at all.

"Kirry's coming this morning," he added. "I have to pick her up at the airport at noon."

Jodie only smiled. "Margie's hoping she'll help her with a market for her designs."

"I think she'll try," he said conservatively. "Eat breakfast," he said. "You can't go all day without food."

"I don't have time," she repeated, starting on another batch of canapés. "Unless you want to sacrifice yourself in a bowl of dough?" she offered, extending the bowl with a mischievous smile.

His green eyes twinkled affectionately in spite of himself. "No, thanks."

"I didn't think so."

He watched her work while he ate, nebulous thoughts racing through his mind. Jodie was so much a part of his life that he never felt discomfort when they were together. He had a hard time with strangers. He appeared to be stoic and aloof, but in fact he was an introvert who didn't quite know how to mix with people who weren't in law enforcement. Like Jodie herself, he considered. She was almost painfully shy around people she didn't know — and tonight, she was going to be thrown in headfirst with a crowd she probably wouldn't even like.

Kirry's friends were social climbers, high society. Alexander himself wasn't comfortable with them, and Jodie certainly wouldn't be. They were into expensive cars, European vacations, diamonds, investments, and they traveled in circles that included some of the most famous people alive, from movie stars to Formula 1 race car drivers, to financial geniuses, playwrights and authors. They classified their friends by wealth and status, not by character. In their world, right and wrong didn't even exist.

"You're not going to like this crowd," he said aloud.

She glanced at him. "I'll be in the kitchen most of the time," she said easily, "or helping serve."

He looked outraged. "You're a guest, not the kitchen help!"

"Don't be absurd," she murmured absently, "I haven't even got the right clothes to wear to Kirry's sort of party. I'd be an embarrassment."

He set his coffee cup down with muted force. "Then why the hell did you come in the first place?" he asked.

"Margie asked me to," she said simply.

He got up and went out without another word. Jodie was going to regret this visit. He was sorry Margie had insisted that she come.

The party was in full swing. Alexander had picked up Kirry at the airport and lugged her suitcases up to the second guest room, down the hall from Jodie's. Kirry, blond and svelte and from a wealthy background was like the Cobbs, old money and family ties. She looked at Jodie without seeing her, and talked only to Margie and Alexander during lunch. Fortunately there were plenty of other people there who didn't mind talking to Jodie, especially an elderly couple apparently rolling in wealth to judge by the diamonds the matron was decked out in.

After lunch, Kirry had Alexander drive her into town and Jodie silently excused herself and escaped to the kitchen.

She had a nice little black dress, off the rack at a local department store, and high heels to match, which she wore to the party. But it was hidden under the big apron she wore most of the evening, heating and arranging canapés and washing dishes and crystal glasses in between uses.

It was almost ten o'clock before she was able to join Margie and her friends. But by then, Margie was hanging on to Kirry like a bat, with Alexander nearby, and Jodie couldn't get near her.

She stood in a corner by herself, wishing that Derek hadn't run from this weekend, so that she'd at least have someone to talk to. But that wasn't happening. She started talking to the elderly matron she'd sat beside at lunch, but another couple joined them and mentioned their week in Paris, and a mutual friend, and Jodie was out of her depth. She moved to another circle, but they were discussing annuities and investments, and she knew nothing to contribute to that discussion, either.

Alexander noticed, seething, that she was alone most of the evening. He started to get up, but Kirry moved closer and clung to his sleeve while Margie talked about her latest collection and offered to show it to Kirry in the morning. Kirry was very possessive. They weren't involved, as he'd been with other women. Perhaps that was why she was reluctant to let him move away. She hated the very thought of any other woman looking at him. That possessiveness was wearing thin. She was beautiful and she carried herself well, but she had an attitude he didn't like, and she was positively rude to any of his colleagues that spoke to him when they were together. Not that she had any idea what Alexander actually did for a living. He was independently wealthy and people in his and Margie's circle of friends assumed that the ranch was his full-time occupation. He'd taught Jodie and Margie never to mention that he worked in Drug Enforcement. They could say that he dabbled in security work, if they liked, but nothing more. When he'd started out with the DEA, he'd done a lot of undercover work. It wasn't politic to let people know that.

Jodie, meanwhile, had discovered champagne. She'd never let herself drink at any of the Cobb parties in the past, but she was feeling particularly isolated tonight, and it was painful. She liked the bubbles, the fragrance of flowers that clung to the exquisite beverage and the delicious taste. So she had three glasses, one after the other, and pretty soon she didn't mind at all that Margie and Alexander's guests were treating her like a barmaid who'd tried to insert herself into their exalted circles.

She noticed that she'd had too much to drink when she walked toward a doorway and ran headfirst into the door facing. She began to giggle softly. Her hair was coming down from its high coiffure, but she didn't care. She took out the circular comb that had held it in place and shook her head, letting the thick, waving wealth of hair fall to her shoulders.

The action caught the eye of a man nearby, a bored race car driver who'd been dragged to this hick party by his wife. He sized up Jodie, and despite the dress that did absolutely nothing for her, he was intrigued.

He moved close, leaning against the door facing she'd hit so unexpectedly.

"Hurt yourself?" he asked in a pleasant deep drawl, faintly accented.

Jodie looked up at the newcomer curiously and managed a lopsided grin. He was a dish, with curly black hair and dancing black eyes, an olive complexion and the body of an athlete.

"Only my hard head," she replied with a chuckle. "Who are you?"

"Francisco," he replied lazily. He lifted his glass to her in a toast. "You're the first person tonight who even asked." He leaned down so that he was eye to eye with her. "I'm a foreigner, you see."

"Are you, really?"

He was enchanted. He laughed, and it wasn't a polite social laugh at all. "I'm from Madrid," he said. "Didn't you notice my accent?"

"I don't speak any foreign languages," she confessed sadly, sipping what was left of her champagne. "I don't understand high finance or read popular novels or know any movie stars, and I've never been on a holiday abroad. So I thought I'd go sit in the kitchen."

He laughed again. "May I join you, then?" he asked.

She looked pointedly at his left hand. There was no ring.

He took a ring out of his slacks pocket and dangled it in front of her. "We don't advertise our commitment at parties. My wife likes it that way. That's my wife," he added with pure disdain, nodding toward a blond woman in a skintight red dress that looked sprayed on. She was leaning against a very handsome blond man.

"She's beautiful," she remarked.

"She's anybody's," he returned coldly. "The man she's stalking is a rising motion picture star. He's poor. She's rich. She's financing his career in return for the occasional loan of his body."

Her eyes almost popped out of her eyelids.

He shook his head. "You're not worldly, are you?" he mused. "I have an open marriage. She does what she pleases. So do I."

"Don't you love her?" she asked curiously.

"One marries for love, you think." He sighed. "What a child you are. I married her because her father owned the company. As his son-in-law, I get to drive the car in competition."

"You're the race car driver!" she exclaimed softly. "Kirry mentioned you were coming."

"Kirry." His lips curled distastefully and he glanced across the room into a pair of cold, angry green eyes above the head of Kirry Dane. "She was last year's diversion," he murmured. "She wanted to be seen at Monaco."

Jodie was surprised by his lack of inhibition. She wondered if Alexander knew about this relationship, or if he cared. She'd never thought whether he bothered asking about his date's previous entanglements.

"Her boyfriend doesn't like me," he murmured absently, and smiled icily, lifting his glass.

Jodie looked behind her. Kirry had turned

away, but Alexander was suddenly making a beeline across the room toward them.

Francisco made a face. "There's one man you don't want to make an enemy of," he confided. "Are you a relation of his, by any chance?"

Jodie laughed a little too loudly. "Good Lord, no." She chuckled. "I'm the cook!"

"I beg your pardon?" he asked.

By that time, Alexander was facing her. He took the crystal champagne flute from her hands and put it gingerly on a nearby table.

"I wasn't going to break it, Alexander," she muttered. "I do know it's Waterford crystal!"

"How many glasses have you had?" he demanded.

"I don't like your tone," she retorted, moving clumsily, so that Francisco had to grab her arm to keep her upright. "I had three glasses. It's not that strong, and I'm not drunk!"

"And ducks don't have feathers," Alexander replied tersely. He caught her other arm and pulled her none too gently from Francisco's grasp. "I'll take care of Jodie. Hadn't you better reacquire your wife?" he added pointedly to the younger man.

Francisco sighed, with a long, wistful appraisal of Jodie. "It seems so," he replied. "Nice to have met you — Jodie, is it?"

Jodie grinned woozily. "It's Jordana, actually, but most people call me Jodie. And I was glad to meet you, too, Francisco! I never met a real race car driver before!"

He started to speak, but it was too late, because Alexander was already marching her out of the room and down the hall.

"Will you stop dragging me around?!" she demanded, stumbling on her high heels.

He pulled her into the dark-paneled library and closed the door with a muted thud. He let go of her arm and glared down at her. "Will you stop trying to seduce married men?" he shot back. "Gomez and his wife are on the cover of half the tabloids in Texas right now," he added bluntly.

"Why?"

"Her father just died and she inherited the car company. She's trying to sell it and her husband is fighting her in court, tooth and nail."

"And they're still married?"

"Apparently, in name, at least. She's pregnant, I hear, with another man's child."

She looked up at him coldly. "Some circles you and Margie travel in," she said with contempt.

"Circles you'd never fit into," he agreed.

"Not hardly," she drawled ungrammatically. "And I wouldn't want to. In my world, people get married and have kids and build a home together." She nodded her head toward the closed door. "Those people in there wouldn't know what a home was if you drew it for them!"

His green eyes narrowed on her face. "You're smashed. Why don't you go to bed?"

She lifted her chin and smiled mistily. "Why don't you come with me?" she purred.

The look on his face would have amused her, if she'd been sober. He just stared, shocked.

She arched her shoulders and made a husky little sound in her throat. She parted her lips and ran her tongue slowly around them, the way she'd read in a magazine article that said men were turned on by it.

Apparently they were. Alexander was staring at her mouth with an odd expression. His chest was rising and falling very quickly. She could see the motion of it through his white shirt and dinner jacket.

She moved closer, draping herself against him as she'd seen that slinky blond woman in the red dress do it. She moved her leg against his and felt his whole body stiffen abruptly.

Her hands went to the front of his shirt under the jacket. She drew her fingers down it, feeling the ripple of muscle. His big hands caught her shoulders, but he wasn't pushing.

"You look at me, but you never see me," she murmured. Her lips brushed against his throat. He smelled of expensive cologne and soap. "I'm not pretty. I'm not sexy. But I would die for you . . . !"

His hard mouth cut off the words. He curled her into his body with a rigid arm at her back, and his mouth opened against her moist, full, parted lips with the fury of a summer storm.

It wasn't premeditated. The feel of her against him had triggered a raging arousal in his muscular body. He went in headfirst, without thinking of the consequences.

If he was helpless, so was she. As he enveloped her against him, her arms slid around his warm body under the jacket and her mouth answered the hunger of his. She made a husky little moan that apparently made matters worse. His mouth became suddenly insistent, as if he heard the need in her soft cry and was doing his best to satisfy the hunger it betrayed.

Her hands lifted to the back of his head

and her fingers dug into his scalp as she arched her body upward in a hopeless plea.

He whispered something that she couldn't understand before he bent and lifted her, with her mouth still trapped under his demanding lips, and carried her to the sofa.

He spread her body onto the cold leather and slid over it, one powerful leg inserting itself between both of hers in a frantic, furious exchange of passion. He'd never known such raging need, not only in himself, but in Jodie. She was liquid in his embrace, yielding to everything he asked without a word being spoken.

He moved slightly, just enough to get his hand in between them. It smoothed over her collarbone and down into the soft dip of her dress, over the lacy bra she was wearing underneath. He felt the hard little nipple in his palm as he increased the insistent pressure of the caress and heard her cry of delight go into his open mouth.

Her hands were on the buttons of his shirt. It was dangerous. It was reckless. She'd incited him to madness, and he couldn't stop. When he felt the buttons give, and her hands speared into the thick hair over his chest, he groaned harshly. His body shivered with desire.

His mouth ground into hers as his leg

moved between hers. One lean hand went under her hips and gathered her up against the fierce arousal of his body, moving her against him in a blatant physical statement of intent.

Jodie's head was spinning. All her dreams of love were coming true. Alexander wanted her! She could feel the insistent pressure of his body over hers. He was kissing her as if he'd die to have her, and she gloried in the fury of his hunger. She relaxed with a husky little laugh and kissed him back languidly, feeling her body melt under him, melt into him. She was on fire, burning with unfamiliar needs, drowning in unfamiliar sensations that made her whole body tingle with pleasure. She lifted her hips against his and gasped at the blatant contact.

Alexander lifted his head and looked at her. His face was a rigid mask. Only his green eyes were alive in it, glittering down at her in a rasping, unsteady silence of merged breathing.

"Don't stop," she whispered, moving her hips again.

He was tempted. It showed. But that iron control wouldn't let him slip into carelessness. She'd been drinking. In fact, she was smashed. He had his own suspicions about her innocence, and they wouldn't shut up.

His body was begging him to forget her lack of experience and give it relief. But his will was too strong. He was the man in control. It was his responsibility to protect her, even from himself.

"You're drunk, Jodie," he said. His voice was faintly unsteady, but it was terse and firm.

"Does it matter?" she asked lazily.

"Don't be ridiculous."

He moved away, getting to his feet. He looked down at her sprawled body in its disheveled dress and he ached all the way to his toes. But he couldn't do this. Not when she was so vulnerable.

She sighed and closed her eyes. It had been so sweet, lying in his arms. She smiled dreamily. Was she dreaming?

"Get up, for God's sake!" he snapped.

When her eyes opened, he was standing her firmly on her feet. "You're going to bed, right now, before you make an utter fool of yourself!"

She blinked, staring up at him. "I can't go to bed. Who'll do the dishes?"

"Jodie!"

She giggled, trying to lean against him. He thrust her away and took her arm, moving her toward the door. "I told Francisco I was the cook. That's me," she drawled cheerfully. "Cook, bottle-washer, best friend and household slave." She laughed louder.

He propelled her out the door, back down the hall toward the staircase, and urged her up it. She was still giggling a little too loudly for comfort, but the noise of the music from the living room covered it nicely.

He got her to the guest room she was occupying and put her inside. "Go to bed," he said through his teeth.

She leaned against the door facing, totally at sea. "You could come inside," she murmured wickedly. "There's a bed."

"You need one," he agreed tersely. "Go get in it."

"Always bossing me around," she sighed. "Don't you like kissing me, Alexander?"

"You're going to hate yourself in the morning," he assured her.

She yawned, her mind going around in circles, like the room. "I think I'll go to bed now."

"Great idea."

He started to walk out.

"Could you send Francisco up, please?" she taunted. "I'd like to lie down and discuss race cars with him."

"In your dreams!" he said coldly.

He actually slammed the door, totally out of patience, self-control and tact. He waited a minute, to make sure she didn't try to come back out. But there was only the sound of slow progress toward the bed and a sudden loud whoosh. When he opened the door again and peeked in, she was lying facedown in her dress on the covers, sound asleep. He closed the door again, determined not to get close to her a second time. He went back to the party, feeling as if he'd had his stomach punched. He couldn't imagine what had possessed him to let Jodie tempt him into indiscretion. His lack of control worried him so much that he was twice as attentive to Kirry as he usually was.

When he saw her up to her room, after the party was over, he kissed her with intent. She was perfectly willing, but his body let him down. He couldn't manage any interest at all.

"You're just tired," she assured him with a worldly smile. "We have all the time in the world. Sleep tight."

"Sure. You, too."

He left her and went back downstairs. He was restless, angry at his attack of impotence with the one woman who was capable of curing it. Or, at least, he imagined she was. He and Kirry had never been lovers, although they'd come close at one time. Now, she was a pleasant companion from time to time, a bauble to show off, to take around town. It infuriated him that he could be whole with Jodie, who was almost certainly a virgin, and he couldn't even function with a sophisticated woman like Kirry. Maybe it was his age.

The rattle of plates caught his attention. He moved toward the sound and found a distressed Margie in the kitchen trying to put dishes in the dishwasher.

"That doesn't look right," he commented with a frown when he noticed the lack of conformity in the way she was tossing plates and bowls and cups and crystal all together. "You'll break the crystal."

She glared at him. "Well, what do I know about washing dishes?" she exclaimed. "That's why we have Jessie!"

He cocked his head. "You're out of sorts."

She pushed back her red-tinged dark hair angrily. "Yes, I'm out of sorts! Kirry said she doesn't think I'm ready to show my collection yet. She said her store had shows booked for the rest of the year, and she couldn't help me!"

"All that buttering up and dragging Jodie down here to work, for nothing," he said sarcastically.

"Where is Jodie?" she demanded. "I haven't seen her for two hours, and here's all this work that isn't getting done except by me!"

He leaned back against the half open door and stared at his sister. "She's passed out on her bed, dead drunk," he said distastefully. "After trying to seduce the world's number one race car driver, and then me."

Margie stood up and stared back. "You?"

"I wish I could impress on you how tired I am of finding Jodie underfoot every time I walk into my own house," he said coldly. "We can't have a party without her, we can't have a holiday without her. My own birthday means an invitation! Why can't you just hire a cook when you need one instead of landing me with your erstwhile best friend?"

"I thought you liked Jodie, a little," Margie stammered.

"She's blue collar, Margie," he persisted, still smarting under his loss of control and furious that Jodie was responsible for it. "She'll never fit in our circles, no matter how much you try to force her into them. She was telling people tonight that she was the cook, and it's not far wrong. She's a social disaster with legs. She knows nothing about our sort of lifestyle, she can't carry on a decent conversation and she dresses like a homeless person. It's an embarrassment to have her here!"

Margie sighed miserably. "I hope you haven't said things like that to her, Lex," she worried. "She may not be an upper class sort of person, but she's sweet and kind, and she doesn't gossip. She's the only real friend I've ever had. Not that I've behaved much like one," she added sadly.

"You should have friends in your own class," he said coldly. "I don't want Jodie invited down here again," he added firmly, holding up a hand when Margie tried to speak. "I mean it. You find some excuse, but you keep her away from here. I'm not going to be stalked by your bag lady of a friend. I don't want her underfoot at any more holidays, and God forbid, at my birthday party! If you want to see her, drive to Houston, fly to Houston, stay in Houston! But don't bring her here anymore."

"Did she really try to seduce you?" Margie wondered aloud.

"I don't want to talk about it," he said flatly. "It was embarrassing."

"She'll probably be horrified when she wakes up and remembers what happened. Whatever did," Margie added, fishing.

"I'll be horrified for months myself. Kirry is my steady girl," he added deliberately. "I'm not hitting on some other woman behind her back, and Jodie should have known it. Not that it seemed to matter to her, about me or the married racer."

"She's never had a drink, as far as I know," Margie ventured gently. "She's not like our mother, Lex."

His face closed up. Jodie's behavior had aroused painful memories of his mother, who drank often, and to excess. She was a constant embarrassment anytime people came to the house, and she delighted in embarrassing her son any way possible. Jodie's unmanageable silliness brought back nightmares.

"There's nothing in the world more disgusting than a drunk woman," he said aloud. "Nothing that makes me sicker to my stomach."

Margie closed the dishwasher and started it. There was a terrible cracking sound. The crystal! She winced. "I don't care what's broken. I'm not a cook. I can't wash dishes. I'm a dress designer!"

"Hire help for Jessie," he said.

"Okay," she said, giving in. "I won't invite Jodie back again. But how do I tell her, Lex? She's never going to understand. And it will hurt her."

He knew that. He couldn't bear to know it. His face hardened. "Just keep her away from me. I don't care how."

"I'll think of something," Margie said weakly.

Outside in the hall, a white-faced Jodie was stealthily making her way back to the staircase. She'd come down belatedly to do the dishes, still tingling hours after Alexander's feverish lovemaking. She'd been floating, delirious with hope that he might have started to see her in a different light. And then she'd heard what he said. She'd heard every single word. She disgusted him. She was such a social disaster, in fact, that he never wanted her to come to the house again. She'd embarrassed him and made a fool of herself.

He was right. She'd behaved stupidly, and now she was going to pay for it by being an outcast. The only family she had no longer wanted her.

She went back to her room, closed the door quietly, and picked up the telephone. She changed her airplane ticket for an early-morning flight.

The next morning, she went to Margie's room at daybreak. She hadn't slept a wink. She'd packed and changed her clothes, and now she was ready to go.

"Will you drive me to the airport?" she asked her sleepy friend. "Or do you want me to ask Johnny?"

Margie sat up, blinking. Then she remembered Lex's odd comments and her own shame at how she'd treated her best friend. She flushed.

"I'll drive you," Margie said at once. "But don't you want to wait until after breakfast?" She flushed again, remembering that Jodie would have had to cook it.

"I'm not hungry. There's leftover sausage and bacon in the fridge, along with some biscuits. You can just heat them up. Alexander can cook eggs to go with them," she added, almost choking on his name.

Margie felt guilty. "You're upset," she ventured.

Keeping quiet was the hardest thing Jodie had ever done. "I got drunk last night and did some . . . really stupid things," she summarized. "I'd just like to go home, Margie. Okay?"

Margie tried not to let her relief show. Jodie was leaving without a fuss. Lex would be pleased, and she'd be off the hook. She smiled. "Okay. I'll just get dressed, and then we'll go!"

FOUR

If running away seemed the right thing to do, actually doing it became complicated the minute Jodie went down the staircase with her suitcase.

The last thing she'd expected was to find the cause of her flight standing in the hall watching her. She ground her teeth together to keep from speaking.

Alexander was leaning against the banister, and he looked both uncomfortable and concerned when he saw Jodie's pale complexion and swollen eyelids.

He stood upright, scowling. "I'm driving Kirry back to Houston this afternoon," he said at once, noting Jodie's suitcase. "You can ride with us."

Jodie forced a quiet smile. Her eyes didn't quite meet his. "Thanks for the offer, Alexander, but I have an airplane ticket."

"Then I'll drive you to the airport," he added quietly.

Her face tightened. She swallowed down her hurt. "Thanks, but Margie's already dressed and ready to go. And we have some things to talk about on the way," she added before he could offer again.

He watched her uneasily. Jodie was acting like a fugitive evading the police. She wouldn't meet his eyes, or let him near her. He'd had all night to regret his behavior, and he was still blaming her for it. He'd overreacted. He knew she'd had a crush on him at one time. He'd hurt her with his cold rejection. She'd been drinking. It hadn't been her fault, but he'd blamed her for the whole fiasco. He felt guilty because of the way she looked.

Before he could say anything else, Margie came bouncing down the steps. "Okay, I'm ready! Let's go," she told Jodie.

"I'm right behind you. So long, Alexander," she told him without looking up past his top shirt button.

He didn't reply. He stood watching until the front door closed behind her. He still didn't understand his own conflicting emotions. He'd hoped to have some time alone with Jodie while he explored this suddenly changed relationship between them. But she was clearly embarrassed about her behavior the night before, and she was running scared. Probably letting her go was the best way to handle it. After a few days, he'd go to see her at the office and smooth things over. He couldn't bear having her look that way and knowing he was responsible for it. Regardless of his burst of bad temper, he cared about Jodie. He didn't want her to be hurt.

"You look very pale, Jodie," Margie commented when she walked her best friend to the security checkpoint. "Are you sure you're all right?"

"I'm embarrassed about how I acted last night, that's all," she assured her best friend. "How did you luck out with Kirry, by the way?"

"Not too well," she replied with a sigh. "And I think I broke all the crystal by putting it in the dishwasher."

"I'm sorry I wasn't able to do that for you," Jodie apologized.

"It's not your fault. Nothing is your fault." Margie looked tormented. "I was going to ask you down to Lex's birthday party next month . . ."

"Margie, I can't really face Alexander right now, okay?" she interrupted gently, and saw the relief plain on the taller woman's face. "So I'm going to make myself scarce for a little while."

"That might be best," Margie had to admit.

Jodie smiled. "Thanks for asking me to the party," she managed. "I had a good time."

That was a lie, and they both knew it.

"I'll make all this up to you one day, I promise I will," Margie said unexpectedly, and hugged Jodie, hard. "I'm not much of a friend, Jodie, but I'm going to change. I am. You'll see."

"I wouldn't be much of a friend if I wanted to remake you," Jodie replied, smiling. "I'll see you around, Margie," she added enigmatically, and left before Margie could ask what she meant.

It was a short trip back to Houston. Jodie fought tears all the way. She couldn't remember anything hurting so much in all her life. Alexander couldn't bear the sight of her. He didn't want her around. She made him sick. She . . . disgusted him.

Most of her memories of love swirled around Alexander Cobb. She'd daydreamed about him even before she realized her feelings had deepened into love. She treasured unexpected meetings with him, she tingled just from having him smile at her. But all that had been a lie. She was a responsibility he took seriously, like his job. She meant nothing more than that to him. It was a painful realization, and it was going to take time for the hurt to lessen.

But for the moment it was too painful to bear. She drew the air carrier's magazine out of its pocket in the back of the seat ahead of her and settled back to read it. By the time she finished, the plane was landing. She walked through the Houston concourse with a new resolution. She was going to forget Alexander. It was time to put away the past and start fresh.

Alexander was alone in the library when his sister came back from the airport.

He went out into the hall to meet her. "Did she say anything to you?" he asked at once.

Surprised by the question, and his faint anxiety, she hesitated. "About what?"

He glowered down at her. "About why she was leaving abruptly. I know her ticket was for late this afternoon. She must have changed it."

"She said she was too embarrassed to face you," Margie replied.

"Anything else?" he persisted.

"Not really." She felt uneasy herself. "You

know Jodie. She's painfully shy, Lex. She doesn't drink, ever. I guess whatever happened made her ashamed of herself and uncomfortable around you. She'll get over it in time."

"Do you think so?" he wondered aloud.

"What are you both doing down here?" Kirry asked petulantly with a yawn. She came down the staircase in a red silk gown and black silk robe and slippers, her long blond hair sweeping around her shoulders. "I feel as if I haven't even slept. Is breakfast ready?"

Margie started. "Well, Jessie isn't here," she began.

"Where's that little cook who was at the party last night?" she asked carelessly. "Why can't she make breakfast?"

"Jodie's not a cook," Alexander said tersely. "She's Margie's best friend."

Kirry's eyebrows arched. "She looked like a lush to me," Kirry said unkindly. "People like that should never drink. Is she too hung over to cook, then?"

"She's gone home," Margie said, resenting Kirry's remarks.

"Then who's going to make toast and coffee for me?" Kirry demanded. "I have to have breakfast."

"I can make toast," Margie said, turning.

She wanted Kirry's help with her collection, but she disliked the woman intensely.

"Then I'll get dressed. Want to come up and do my zip, Lex?" Kirry drawled.

"No," he said flatly. "I'll make coffee." He went into the kitchen behind Margie.

Kirry stared after him blankly. He'd never spoken to her in such a way before, and Margie had been positively rude. They shouldn't drink, either, she was thinking as she went back upstairs to dress. Obviously it was hangovers and bad tempers all around this morning.

Two weeks later, Jodie sat in on a meeting between Brody and an employee of their information systems section who had been rude and insulting to a fellow worker. It was Brody's job as Human Resources generalist to oversee personnel matters, and he was a diplomat. It gave Jodie the chance to see what sort of duties she would be expected to perform if she moved up from Human Resources generalist to manager.

"Mr. Koswalski, this is Ms. Clayburn, my administrative assistant. She's here to take notes," he added.

Jodie was surprised, because she thought she was there to learn the job. But she smiled and pulled out her small pad and pen, perching it on her knee.

"You've had a complaint about me, haven't you?" Koswalski asked with a sigh.

Brody's eyebrows arched. "Well, yes . . ."

"One of our executives hired a systems specialist with no practical experience in oil exploration," Koswalski told him. "I was preparing an article for inclusion in our quarterly magazine and the system went down. She was sent to repair it. She saw my article and made some comments about the terms I used, and how unprofessional they sounded. Obviously she didn't understand the difference between a rigger and a rough-neck. When I tried to explain, she accused me of talking down to her and walked out." He threw up his hands. "Sir, I wasn't rude, and I wasn't uncooperative. I was trying to teach her the language of the industry."

Brody looked as if he meant to say some-thing, but he glanced at Jodie and cleared his throat instead. "You didn't call her names, Mr. Koswalski?"

"No, sir, I did not," the young man replied courteously. "But she did call me several. Besides that, quite frankly, she had a glazed look in her eyes and a red nose." His face tautened. "Mr. Vance, I've seen too many people who use drugs to mistake signs of drug use. She didn't repair the system, she made matters worse. I had to call in another specialist to undo her damage. I have his name, and his assignment," he added, producing a slip of paper, which he handed to Brody. "I'm sorry to make a counter-charge of incompetence against another employee, but my integrity is at stake."

Brody took the slip of paper and read the name. He looked at the younger man again. "I know this technician. He's the best we have. He'll confirm what you just told me?"

"He will, Mr. Vance."

Brody nodded. "I'll check with him and make some investigation of your charges. You'll be notified when we have a resolution. Thank you, Mr. Koswalski."

"Thank you, Mr. Vance," the young man replied, standing. "I enjoy my job very much. If I lose it, it should be on merit, not lies."

"I quite agree," Brody replied. "Good day."

"Good day." Koswalski left, very dignified.

Brody turned to Jodie. "How would you characterize our Mr. Koswalski?"

"He seems sincere, honest, and hardworking."

He nodded. "He's here on time every morning, never takes longer than he has for lunch, does any task he's given willingly and without protest, even if it means working late hours."

He picked up a file folder. "On the other hand, the systems specialist, a Ms. Burgen, has been late four out of five mornings she's worked here. She misses work on Mondays every other week. She complains if she's asked to do overtime, and her work is unsatisfactory." He looked up. "Your course of action, in my place?"

"I would fire her," she said.

He smiled slowly. "She has an invalid mother and a two-year-old son," he said surprisingly. "She was fired from her last job. If she loses this one, she faces an uncertain future."

She bit her lower lip. It was one thing to condone firing an incompetent employee, but given the woman's home life the decision was uncomfortable.

"If you take my place, you'll be required to make such recommendations. In fact, you'll be required to make them to me," he added. "You can't wear your heart on your sleeve. You work for a business that depends on its income. Incompetent employees will cost us time, money, and possibly even clients. No business can exist that way for long."

She looked up at him with sad eyes. "It's not a nice job, Brody."

He nodded. "It's like gardening. You have to separate the weeds from the vegetables. Too many weeds, no more vegetables."

"I understand." She looked at her pad. "So what will you recommend?" she added.

"That our security section make a thorough investigation of her job performance," he said. "If she has a drug problem that relates to it, she'll be given the choice of counseling and treatment or separation. Unless she's caught using drugs on the job, of course," he added coolly. "In that case, she'll be arrested."

She knew she was growing cold inside. What had sounded like a wonderful position was weighing on her like a rock.

"Jodie, is this really what you want to do?" he asked gently, smiling. "Forgive me, but you're not a hardhearted person, and you're forever making excuses for people. It isn't the mark of a manager."

"I'm beginning to realize that," she said quietly. She searched his eyes. "Doesn't it bother you, recommending that people lose their jobs?"

"No," he said simply. "I'm sorry for them, but not sorry enough to risk my paycheck and yours keeping them on a job they're not qualified to perform. That's business, Jodie."

"I suppose so." She toyed with her pad. "I was a whiz with computers in business college," she mused. "I didn't want to be a systems specialist because I'm not mechanically-minded, but I could do anything with software." She glanced at him. "Maybe I'm in the wrong job to begin with. Maybe I should have been a software specialist."

He grinned. "If you decide, eventually, that you'd like to do that, write a job description, give it to your Human Resources manager, and apply for the job," he counseled.

"You're kidding!"

"I'm not. It's how I got my job," he confided.

"Well!"

"You don't have to fire software," he reminded her. "And if it doesn't work, it won't worry your conscience to toss it out. But all this is premature. You don't have to decide right now what you want to do. Besides," he added with a sigh, "I may not even get that promotion I'm hoping for."

"You'll get it," she assured him. "You're terrific at what you do, Brody."

"Do you really think so?" he asked, and

seemed to care about her reply.

"I certainly do."

He smiled. "Thanks. Cara doesn't think much of my abilities, I'm afraid. I suppose it's because she's so good at marketing. She gets promotions all the time. And the travel . . . ! She's out of town more than she's in, but she loves it. She was in Mexico last week and in Peru the week before that. Imagine! I'd love to go to Mexico and see Chichen Itza." He sighed.

"So would I. You like archaeology?" she fished.

He grinned. "Love it. You?"

"Oh, yes!"

"There's a museum exhibit of Mayan pottery at the art museum," he said enthusiastically. "Cara hates that sort of thing. I don't suppose you'd like to go with me to see it next Saturday?"

Next Saturday. Alexander's birthday. She'd mourned for the past two weeks since she'd come back from the Cobbs' party, miserable and hurting. But she wouldn't be invited to his birthday party, and she wouldn't go even if she was.

"I'd love to," she said with a beaming smile. "But . . . won't your girlfriend mind?"

He frowned. "I don't know." He looked down at her. "We, uh, don't have to advertise it, do we?"

She understood. It was a little uncomfortable going out with a committed man, but it wasn't as if he were married or anything. Besides, his girlfriend treated him like dirt. She wouldn't.

"No, we don't," she agreed. "I'll look forward to it."

"Great!" He beamed, too. "I'll phone you Friday night and we'll decide where and when to meet, okay?"

"Okay!"

She was on a new track, a new life, and she felt like a new person. She'd started going to a retro coffeehouse in the evenings, where they served good coffee and people read poetry on stage or played folk music with guitars. Jodie fit right in with the artsy crowd. She'd even gotten up for the first time and read one of her poems, a sad one about rejected love that Alexander had inspired. Everyone applauded, even the owner, a man named Johnny. The boost of confidence she felt made her less inhibited, and the next time she read her poetry, she wasn't afraid of the crowd. She was reborn. She was the new, improved Jodie, who could conquer the world. And now Brody wanted to date her. She was delighted.

That feeling lasted precisely two hours. She came back in after lunch to find Alexander Cobb perched on her desk, in her small cubicle, waiting for her.

She hadn't had enough time to get over her disastrous last meeting with him. She wanted to turn and run, but that wasn't going to work. He'd already spotted her.

She walked calmly to her desk — although her heart was doing cartwheels — and put her purse in her lower desk drawer.

"Hello, Alexander," she said somberly. "What can I do for you?"

Her attitude sent him reeling. Jodie had always been unsettled and full of joy when she came upon him unexpectedly. He didn't realize how much he'd enjoyed the headlong reaction until it wasn't there anymore.

He stared at her across the desk, puzzled and disturbed. "What happened wasn't anybody's fault," he said stiffly. "Don't wear yourself out regretting it."

She relaxed a little, but only a little. "I drank too much. I won't do it a second time," she assured him. "How's Margie?"

"Quiet," he said. The one word was alarming. Margie was never quiet.

"Why?" she asked.

Shrugging, he picked up a paper clip from her desk and studied it. "She can't get anywhere with her designs. She expected immediate success, and she can't even get a foot in the door."

"I'm sorry. She's really good."

He nodded and his green eyes met hers narrowly. "I need to talk to you," he said. "Can you meet me downstairs at the coffee bar when you get off from work?"

She didn't want to, and it was obvious. "Couldn't you just phone me at home?" she countered.

He scowled. "No. I can't discuss this over the phone." She was still hesitating. "Do you have other plans?" he asked.

She shook her head. "No. I don't want to miss my bus."

"I can drive you . . ."

"No! I mean —" she lowered her voice "— no, I won't put you to any trouble. There are two buses. The second runs an hour after the first one."

"It won't take an hour," he assured her. But he felt as if something was missing from their conversation. She didn't tease him, taunt him, antagonize him. In fact, she looked very much as if she wanted to avoid him altogether.

"All right, then," she said, sitting down at her desk. "I'll see you there about five after five."

He nodded, pausing at the opening of the cubicle to look back at her. It was a bad time to remember the taste of her full, soft mouth under his. But he couldn't help it. She was wearing a very businesslike dark suit with a pale pink blouse, her long hair up in a bun. She should have looked like a businesswoman, but she was much too vulnerable, too insecure, to give that image. She didn't have the self-confidence to rate a higher job, but he couldn't tell her that. Jodie had a massive inferiority complex. The least thing hurt her. As he'd hurt her.

The muscles in his jaw tautened. "This doesn't suit you," he said abruptly, nodding around the sterile little glass and wood cage they kept her in. "Won't they even let you have a potted plant?"

She was aghast at the comment. He never made personal remarks. She shifted restlessly in her chair. "It isn't dignified," she stammered.

He moved a step closer. "Jodie, a job shouldn't mimic jail. If you don't like what you do, where you do it, you're wasting the major part of your life."

She knew that. She tasted panic when she swallowed. But jobs were thin on the ground and she had the chance for advancement in this one. She put to the back of her mind

Brody's comments on her shortcomings as a manager.

"I like my job very much," she lied.

His eyes slid over her with something like possession. "No, you don't. Pity. You have a gift for computer programming. I'll bet you haven't written a single routine since you've been here."

Her face clenched. "Don't you have something to do? Because I'm busy."

"Suit yourself. As soon after five as you can make it, please," he said, adding deliberately, "I have a dinner date."

With Kirry. Always with Kirry. She knew it. She hated Kirry. She hated him, too. But she smiled. "No problem. See you." She turned on her computer and pulled up her memo file to see what tasks were upcoming. She ignored Alexander, who gave her another long, curious appraisal before he left her alone.

She felt the sting of his presence all the way to her poor heart. He was so much a part of her life that it was like being amputated when she thought of a lifetime without his complicated presence.

For the first time, she thought about moving to another city. Ritter Oil Corporation had a headquarters office in Tulsa, Oklahoma. Perhaps she could get a transfer there . . . and do what, she asked herself? She was barely qualified for the predominantly clerical job she was doing now, and painfully unqualified for firing people, even if they deserved it. She'd let her pride force her into taking this job, because Alexander kept asking when she was going to start working after her graduation from business college. He probably hadn't meant that he thought she was taking advantage of his financial help — but she took it that way. So she went to work for the first company that offered her a job, just to shut him up.

In retrospect, she should have looked a little harder. She'd been under consideration for a job with the local police department, as a computer specialist. She had the skills to write programs, to restructure software. She was a whiz at opening protected files, finding lost documents, tracking down suspicious e-mails and finding ways to circumvent write-protected software. Her professor had recommended her for a career in law enforcement as a cyber crime specialist, but she'd jumped at the first post-college job that came her way.

Now here she was, stuck in a dead-end job that she didn't even like, kept in a cubicle like a box of printer paper and only taken out when some higher-up needed her to take a letter or organize a schedule, or compile his notes . . .

She had a vision of herself as a cardboard box full of supplies and started giggling.

Another administrative assistant stuck her head in the cubicle. "Better keep it down," she advised softly. "They've had a complaint about the noise levels in here."

"I'm only laughing to myself," Jodie protested, shocked.

"They want us quiet while we're working. No personal phone calls, no talking to ourselves — and there's a new memo about the length of time people are taking in the bathroom . . ."

"Oh, good God!" Jodie burst out furiously.

The other woman put a feverish hand to her lips and looked around nervously. "Shhh!" she cautioned.

Jodie stood up and gave the woman her best military salute.

Sadly the vice president in charge of personnel was walking by her cubicle at the time. He stopped, eyeing both women suspiciously.

Already in trouble, and not giving a damn anymore, Jodie saluted him, too.

Surprisingly he had to suppress a smile. He wiped it off quickly. "Back to work, girls," he cautioned and kept walking.

The other woman moved closer. "Now see what you've done!" she hissed. "We'll both be on report!"

"If he tries to put me on report, I'll put him on report as well," Jodie replied coolly. "Nobody calls me a 'girl' in a working office!"

The other woman threw up her hands and walked out.

Jodie turned her attention back to her chores and put the incident out of her mind. But it was very disturbing to realize how much authority the company had over her working life, and she didn't like it. She wondered if old man Ritter, the head of the corporation, encouraged such office politics. From what she'd heard about him, he was something of a renegade. He didn't seem to like rules and regulations very much, but, then, he couldn't be everywhere. Maybe he didn't even know the suppressive tactics his executives used to keep employees under control here.

Being cautioned never to speak was bad enough, and personalization of cubicles was strictly forbidden by company policy. But to have executives complain about the time employees spent in the bathroom made Jodie furious. She had a girlfriend who was a diabetic, and made frequent trips to the rest room in school. Some teachers had made it very difficult for her until her parents had requested a teacher conference to explain their daughter's health problem. She had a feeling no sort of conference would help at this job.

She went back to work, but the day had been disturbing in more ways than one.

At exactly five minutes past quitting time, she walked into the little coffee shop downstairs. Alexander had a table, and he was waiting for her. He'd already ordered the French Vanilla cappuccino she liked so much, along with chocolate biscotti.

She was surprised by his memory of her preferences. She draped her old coat over the empty chair at the corner table and sat down. Fortunately the shop wasn't crowded, as it was early in the evening, and there were no customers anywhere near them.

"Right on time," Alexander noted, checking his expensive wristwatch.

"I usually am," she said absently, sipping her cappuccino. "This is wonderful," she added with a tiny smile.

He seemed puzzled. "Don't you come here often?"

"Actually, it's not something I can fit into

my budget," she confessed.

Now it was shock that claimed his features. "You make a good salary," he commented.

"If you want to rent someplace with good security, it costs more," she told him. "I have to dress nicely for work, and that costs, too. By the time I add in utilities and food and bus fare, there isn't a lot left. We aren't all in your income tax bracket, Alexander," she added without rancor.

He let his attention wander to his own cappuccino. He sipped it quietly.

"I never think of you as being in a different economic class," he said.

"Don't you?" She knew better, and her thoughts were bitter. She couldn't forget what she'd overheard him say to his sister, that she was only blue collar and she didn't fit in with them.

He sat up straight. "Something's worrying you," he said flatly. "You're not the same. You haven't been since the party."

Her face felt numb. She couldn't lower her pride enough to tell him what she'd overheard. It was just too much, on top of everything else that had gone haywire lately.

"Why can't you talk to me?" he persisted.

She looked up at him with buried resentments, hurt pride, and outraged sentiment plain in her cold eyes. "It would be like talking to the floor," she said. "If you're here, it's because you want something. So, what is it?"

His expression was eloquent. He sipped cappuccino carefully and then put the delicate cup in its saucer with precision.

"Why do you think I want something?"

She felt ancient. "Margie invites me to parties so that I can cook and clean up the kitchen, if Jessie isn't available," she said in a tone without inflection. "Or if she's sick and needs nursing. You come to see me if you need something typed, or a computer program tweaked, or some clue traced back to an ISP online. Neither of you ever come near me unless I'm useful."

His breath caught. "Jodie, it's not like that!"

She looked at him steadily. "Yes, it is. It always has been. I'm not complaining," she added at once. "I don't know what I would have done if it hadn't been for you and Margie. I owe you more than I can ever repay in my lifetime. It's just that since you're here, there's something you need done, and I know it. No problem. Tell me what you want me to do."

His eyes closed and opened again, on a pained expression. It was true. He and Margie had used her shamelessly, but without realizing they were so obvious. He hated the thought.

"It's a little late to develop a conscience," she added with a faint smile. "It's out of character, anyway. Come on. What is it?"

He toyed with his biscotti. "I told you that we're tracking a link to the drug cartel."

She nodded.

"In your company," he added.

"You said I couldn't help," she reminded him.

"Well, I was wrong. In fact, you're the only one who can help me with this."

A few weeks ago, she'd have joked about getting a badge or a gun. Now she just waited for answers. The days of friendly teasing were long gone.

He met her searching gaze. "I want you to pretend that we're developing a relationship," he said, "so that I have a reason to hang around your division."

She didn't react. She was proud of herself. It would have been painfully easy to dump the thick, creamy cappuccino all over his immaculate trousers and anoint him with the cream.

His eyebrow jerked. "Yes, you're right, I'm using you. It's the only way I can find to do surveillance. I can't hang around Jasper or

106

people will think I'm keen on him!"

That thought provoked a faint smile. "His wife wouldn't like it."

He shrugged. "Will you do it?"

She hesitated.

He anticipated that. He took out a photograph and slid it across the table to her.

She picked it up. It was of two young boys, about five or six, both smiling broadly. They had thick, straight black hair and black eyes and dark complexions. They looked Latin. She looked back up at Alexander with a question in her eyes.

"Their mother was tired of having drug users in her neighborhood. They met in an abandoned house next door to her. There were frequent disputes, usually followed by running gun battles. The dealer who made the house his headquarters got ambitious. He decided to double-cross the new drug leadership that came in after Manuel Lopez's old territory was finally divided," he said carelessly. "Mama Garcia kept a close eye on what was going on, and kept the police informed. She made the fatal error of telling her infrequent neighbor that his days in her neighborhood were numbered. He told his supplier.

"All this got back to the new dealer network. So when they came to take out the double-crossing dealer, they were quite particular about where they placed the shots. They knew where Mama Garcia lived, and they targeted her along with their rival. Miguel and Juan were hit almost twenty times with automatic weapon fire. They died in the firefight, along with the rebellious dealer. Their mother was wounded and will probably never walk again."

She winced as she looked at the photograph of the two little boys, so happy and smiling. Both dead, over drugs.

He saw her discomfort and nodded. "The local distributor I'm after ordered the hit. He works in this building, in this corporation, in this division." He leaned forward, and she'd never seen him look so menacing. "I'm going to take him out. So, I'll ask you one more time, Jodie. Will you help me?"

FIVE

Jodie groaned inwardly. She knew as she looked one last time at the photograph that she couldn't let a child-killer walk the streets, no matter what the sacrifice to herself.

She handed him back the photograph. "Yes, I'll do it," she said in a subdued tone. "When do I start?"

"Tomorrow at lunch. We'll go out to eat. You can give me the grand tour on the way."

"Okay."

"You still look reluctant," he said with narrowed eyes.

"Brody just asked me out, for the first time," she confessed, trying to sound more despondent than she actually was. It wouldn't hurt to let Alexander know that she wasn't pining over him.

His expression was not easily read. "I thought he was engaged."

She grimaced. "Well, things are cooling

off," she defended herself. "His girlfriend travels all over the world. She just came back from trips to Mexico and Peru, and she doesn't pay Brody much attention even when she's here!" she muttered.

"Peru?" He seemed thoughtful. He studied her quietly for a long moment before he spoke. "They're still engaged, Jodie."

And he thought less of her because she was ignoring another woman's rights. Of course he did. She didn't like the idea, either, and she knew she wasn't going to go out with Brody a week from Saturday. Not now. Alexander made her feel too guilty.

She traced the rim of her china coffee cup. "You're right," she had to admit. "It's just that she treats him so badly," she added with a wistful smile. "He's a sweet man. He's always encouraging me in my job, telling me I can do things, believing in me."

"Which is no damned reason to have an affair with a man," he said furiously. It made him angry to think that another man was trying to uplift Jodie's ego when he'd done nothing but damage to it.

She lowered her voice. "I am not having an affair with him!"

"But you would, if he asked," he said, his eyes as cold as green glass.

She started to argue, then stopped. It

would do no good to argue. Besides, it was her life, and he had no business telling her how to live it.

"How do you want me to act while we're pretending to get involved?" she countered sourly. "Do you want me to throw myself at you and start kissing you when you walk into my cubicle?"

His eyes dilated. "I beg your pardon?"

"Never mind," she said, ruffled. "I'll play it by ear."

He really did seem different, she thought, watching him hesitate uncharacteristically. He drew a diskette in a plastic holder out of his inside jacket pocket and handed it to her.

"Another chore," he added, glancing around to make sure they weren't being observed. "I want you to check out these Web sites, and the e-mail addresses, without leaving footprints. I want to know if they're legitimate and who owns them. They're password protected and in code."

"No problem," she said easily. "I can get behind any firewall they put up."

"Don't leave an address they can trace back to you," he emphasized. "These people won't hesitate to kill children. They wouldn't mind wasting you."

"I get the point. I'm not sloppy." She

slipped the diskette into her purse and finished her coffee. "Anything else?"

"Yes. Margie said to tell you that she's sorry."

Her eyebrows arched. "For what?"

"For everything." He searched her eyes. "And for the record, you don't owe us endless favors, debt or no debt."

She got to her feet. "I know that. I'll have this information for you tomorrow by the time you get here."

He got up, too, catching the bill before she had time to grab it. "My conference, my treat," he said. He stared down at her with an intensity that was disturbing. "You're still keeping something back," he said in a deep, low tone.

"Nothing of any importance," she replied. It was disconcerting that he could read her expressions that well.

His eyes narrowed. "Do you really like working here, Jodie?"

"You're the one who said I needed to stop loafing and get a job," she accused with more bitterness than she realized. "So I got one."

He actually winced. "I said you needed to get your priorities straight," he countered. "Not that you needed to jump into a job you hate."

"I like Brody."

"Brody isn't the damned job," he replied tersely. "You're not cut out for monotony. It will kill your soul."

She knew that; she didn't want to admit it. "Don't you have a hot date?" she asked sarcastically, out of patience with his meddling.

He sighed heavily. "Yes. Why don't you?"

"Men aren't worth the trouble they cause," she lied, turning.

"Oh, you'd know?" he drawled sarcastically. "With your hectic social life?"

She turned, furious. "When Brody's free, look out," she said.

He didn't reply. But he watched her all the way down the hall.

She fumed all the way home. Alexander had such a nerve, she thought angrily. He could taunt her with his conquests, use her to do his decryption work, force her into becoming his accomplice in an investigation . . . !

Wait a minute, she thought suddenly, her hand resting on her purse over the diskette he'd entrusted her with. He had some of the best cyber crime experts in the country on his payroll. Why was he farming out work to an amateur who didn't even work for him?

The answer came in slowly, as she recalled bits and pieces of information she'd heard during the Lopez investigation. She knew people in Jacobsville who kept in touch with her after her move to Houston. Someone had mentioned that there were suspicions of a mole in the law enforcement community, a shadowy figure who'd funneled information to Lopez so that he could escape capture.

Then Alexander's unusual request made sense. He suspected somebody in his organization of working with the drug dealers, and he wanted someone he could trust to do this investigation for him.

She felt oddly touched by his confidence, not only in her ability, but also in her character. He'd refused to let her help him before, but now he was trusting her with explosive information. He was letting her into his life, even on a limited basis. He had to care about her, a little.

Sure he did, she told herself glumly. She was a computer whiz, and he knew it. Hadn't he paid for the college education that had honed those skills? He trusted her ability to manipulate software and track criminal activity through cyberspace. That didn't amount to a declaration of love. She had to stop living in dreams. There was no hope of a future with Alexander. She wasn't even his type. He liked highly intelligent, confident women. He liked professionals. Jodie was more like a mouse. She kept in her little corner, avoiding confrontation, hiding her abilities, speaking only when spoken to, never demanding anything.

She traced the outline of the diskette box through the soft leather of her purse, bought almost new at a yard sale. She pursed her lips. Well, maybe it was time she stopped being everybody's lackey and started standing up for herself. She was smart. She was capable. She could do any job she really wanted to do.

She thought about firing a woman with a dependent elderly mother and child and ground her teeth together. It was becoming obvious that she was never going to enjoy that sort of job.

On the other hand, tracking down criminals was exciting. It made her face flush as she considered how valuable she could be to Alexander in this investigation. She thought of the two little Garcia boys and their poor mother, and her eyes narrowed angrily. She was going to help Alexander catch the animal who'd ordered that depraved execution. And she was just the woman with the skills to do it.

■ ■ ■ ■

Jodie spent most of the evening and the wee hours of the morning tracking down the information Alexander had asked her to find for him. She despaired a time or two, because she ran into one dead end after another. The drug dealers must have cyber experts of their own, and of a high caliber, if they could do this sort of thing.

She finally found a Web site that listed information which was, on the surface, nothing more than advisories about the best sites to find UFO information. But one of the addresses coincided with the material she'd printed out from Alexander's diskette, as a possible link to the drug network. She opened site after site, but she found nothing more than double-talk about possible landing sites and dates. Most covered pages and pages of data, but the last one had only one page of information. It was oddly concise, and the sites were all in a defined area — Texas and Mexico and Peru. Strange, she thought. But, then, Peru was right next door to Colombia. And while drugs and Colombia went together like apples and pie, few people outside law enforcement would connect Peru with drug smuggling.

It was two in the morning, and she was so sleepy that she began to laugh at her own inadequacy. But as she looked at the last site she made sudden sense of the numbers and landing sites. Quickly she printed out the single page of UFO landing sites.

There was a pattern in the listings. It was so obvious that it hit her in the face. She grabbed a pencil and pad and began writing down the numbers. From there, it was a quick move to transpose them with letters. They spelled an e-mail address.

She plugged back into her ISP and changed identities to avoid leaving digital footprints. Then she used a hacker's device to find the source of the e-mail. It originated from a foreign server, and linked directly to a city in Peru. Moreover, a city in Peru near the border with Colombia. She copied down the information without risking leaving it in her hard drive and got out fast.

She folded the sheets of paper covered with her information — because she hadn't wanted to leave anything on her computer that could be accessed if she were online — and placed them in her purse. She smiled sleepily as she climbed into bed with a huge yawn. Alexander, she thought, was going to be impressed.

In fact, he was speechless. He went over the figures in his car in the parking lot on the way to lunch. His eyes met Jodie's and he shook his head.

"This is ingenious," he murmured.

"They did do a good job of hiding information . . ." she agreed.

"No! Your work," he corrected instantly. "This is quality work, Jodie. Quality work. I can't think of anyone who could have done it better."

"Thanks," she said.

"And you're taking notes for Brody Vance," he said with veiled contempt. "He should be working for you."

She chuckled at the thought of Brody with a pad and pen sitting with his legs crossed under a skirt, in front of her desk. "He wouldn't suit."

"You don't suit the job you're doing," he replied. "When this case is solved, I want you to consider switching vocations. Any law enforcement agency with a cyber crime unit would be proud to have you."

Except his, she was thinking, but she didn't say it. A compliment from Alexander was worth something. "I might do that," she said noncommittally.

"I'll put this to good use," he said, sliding the folded sheets into his inside suit pocket. "Where do you want to eat?" he added.

"I usually eat downstairs in the cafeteria. They have a blue plate special . . ."

"Where does your boss have lunch?"

"Brody?" She blinked. "When his girlfriend's in town, he usually goes to a Mexican restaurant, La Rancheria. It's three blocks over near the north expressway," she added.

"I know where it is. What's his girlfriend like?"

She shrugged. "Very dark, very beautiful, very chic. She's District Marketing manager for the whole southwest. She oversees our sales force for the gas and propane distribution network. We sell all over the world, of course, not just in Texas."

"But she travels to Mexico and Peru," he murmured as he turned the Jaguar into traffic.

"She has family in both places," she said disinterestedly. "Her mother was moving from a town in Peru near the Colombian border down to Mexico City, and Cara had to help organize it. That's what she told Brody." She frowned. "Odd, I thought Brody said her mother was dead. But, then,

I didn't really pay attention. I've only seen her a couple of times. She leads Brody around by the nose. He's not very forceful."

"Do you like Mexican food?"

"The real thing, yes," she said with a sigh. "I usually get my chili fix from cans or TV dinners. It's not the same."

"No, it's not."

"You used to love eggs ranchero for breakfast," she commented, and then could have bitten her tongue out for admitting that she remembered his food preferences.

"Yes. You made them for me at four in the morning, the day my father died. Jessie was in tears, so was Margie. Nobody was awake. I'd come from overseas and didn't even have supper. You heard me rattling around in the kitchen trying to make a sandwich," he recalled with a strangely tender smile. "You got up and started cooking. Never said a word, either," he added. "You put the plate in front of me, poured coffee, and went away." He shrugged. "I couldn't have talked to save my life. I was too broken up at losing Dad. You knew that. I never understood how."

"Neither did I," she confessed. She looked out the window. It was a cold day, misting rain. The city looked smoggy. That wasn't surprising. It usually did.

"What is it about Vance that attracts you?" he asked abruptly.

"Brody? Well, he's kind and encouraging, he always makes people feel good about themselves. I like being with him. He's . . . I don't know . . . comfortable."

"Comfortable." He made the word sound insulting. He turned into the parking lot of the Mexican restaurant.

"You asked," she pointed out.

He cut off the engine and glanced at her. "God forbid that a woman should ever find me comfortable!"

"That would take a miracle," she said sweetly, and unfastened her seat belt.

He only laughed.

They had a quiet lunch. Brody wasn't there, but Alexander kept looking around as if he expected the man to materialize right beside the table.

"Are you looking for someone?" she asked finally.

He glanced at her over his dessert, a caramel flan. "I'm always looking for someone," he returned. "It's my job."

She didn't think about what he did for a living most of the time. Of course, the bulge under his jacket where he carried his gun was a dead giveaway, and sometimes he mentioned a case he was working on. Today, their combined efforts on the computer tracking brought it up. But she could go whole days without realizing that he put himself at risk to do the job. In his position, it was inevitable that he would make enemies. Some of them must have been dangerous, but he'd never been wounded.

"Thinking deep thoughts?" he asked her as he registered her expression.

"Not really. This flan is delicious."

"No wonder your boss frequents the place. The food is good, too."

"I really like the way they make coffee . . ."

"Kennedy!" Alexander called to a man just entering the restaurant, interrupting Jodie's comment.

An older man glanced his way, hesitated, and then smiled broadly as he joined them. "Cobb!" he greeted. "Good to see you!"

"I thought you were in New Orleans," Alexander commented.

"I was. Got through quicker than I thought I would. Who's this?" he added with a curious glance at Jodie.

"Jodie's my girl," Alexander said carelessly. "Jodie, this is Bert Kennedy, one of my senior agents."

They shook hands.

"Glad to meet you, Mr. Kennedy."

"Same here, Miss . . . ?"

Alexander ignored the question. Jodie just smiled at him.

"Uh, any luck on the shipyard tip?" Kennedy asked.

Alexander shook his head. "Didn't pan out." He didn't meet the older man's eyes. "We may put a man at Thorn Oil next week," he said in a quiet tone, glancing around to make sure they weren't subject to eavesdroppers. "I'll tell you about it later."

Kennedy had been nervous, but now he relaxed and began to grin. "Great! I'd love to be in on the surveillance," he added. "Unless you have something bigger?"

"We'll talk about it later. See you."

Kennedy nodded, and walked on to a table by the window.

"Is he one of your best men?" she asked Alexander.

"Kennedy is a renegade," he murmured coolly, watching the man from a distance. "He's the bird who brought mercenaries into my drug bust in Jacobsville the year before last, without warning me first. One of their undercover guys almost got killed because we didn't know who he was."

"Eb Scott's men," she ventured.

He nodded. "I was already upset because Manuel Lopez had killed my undercover officer, Walt Monroe. He was my newest agent. I sent him to infiltrate Lopez's organization." His eyes were bleak. "I wanted Lopez. I wanted him badly. The night of the raid, I had no idea that Scott and his gang were even on the place. They were running a Mexican national undercover. If Kennedy knew, he didn't tell me. We could have killed him, or Scott, or any of his men. They weren't supposed to be there."

"I expect Mr. Kennedy lived to regret that decision."

He gave her a cool look. "Oh, he regretted it, all right."

She wasn't surprised that Mr. Kennedy was intimidated by Alexander. Most people were, herself included.

She finished her coffee. "Thanks for lunch," she said. "I really enjoyed it."

He studied her with real interest. "You have exquisite manners," he commented. "Your mother did, too."

She felt her cheeks go hot. "She was a stickler for courtesy," she replied.

"So was your father. They were good people."

"Like your own father."

"I loved him. My mother never forgave him for leaving her for a younger woman," he commented in a rare lapse. "She drank like a fish. Margie and I were stuck with her, because she put on such a good front in court that nobody believed she was a raging alcoholic. She got custody and made us pay for my father's infidelities until she finally died. By then, we were almost grown. We still loved him, though."

She hadn't known the Cobbs' mother very well. Margie had been reluctant to invite her to their home while the older woman was still alive, although Margie spent a lot of time at Jodie's home. Margie and Alexander were very fond of Mr. and Mrs. Clayburn, and they brought wonderful Christmas presents to them every year. Jodie had often wondered just how much damage his mother had done to Alexander in his younger, formative years. It might explain a lot about his behavior from time to time.

"Did you love your mother?" she asked.

He glared at her. "I hated her."

She swallowed. She thought back to the party, to her uninhibited behavior when she'd had those glasses of champagne. She'd brought back terrible memories for Alexander, of his mother, his childhood. Only now did she understand why he'd reacted so violently. No wonder she'd made him sick. He identified her behavior with his mother's. But he'd said other things as well, things she couldn't forget. Things that hurt.

She dropped her eyes and looked at her watch. "I really have to get back," she began.

His hand went across the table to cover hers. "Don't," he said roughly. "Don't look like that! You don't drink normally, not ever. That's why the champagne hit you so hard. I overreacted. Don't let it ruin things between us, Jodie."

She took a slow breath to calm herself. She couldn't meet his eyes. She looked at his mouth instead, and that was worse. It was a chiseled, sensuous mouth and she couldn't stop remembering how it felt to be kissed by it. He was expert. He was over-whelming. She wanted him to drag her into his arms and kiss her blind, and that would never do.

She withdrew her hand with a slow smile. "I'm not holding grudges, Alexander," she reassured him. "Listen, I really have to get back. I've got a diskette full of letters to get out by quitting time."

"All right," he said. "Let's go."

Kennedy raised his hand and waved as they went out. Alexander returned the salute, sliding his hand around Jodie's waist as they left the building. But she noticed that he dropped it the minute they entered the parking lot. He was putting on an act, and she'd better remember it. She'd already been hurt once. There was no sense in inviting more pain from the same source.

He left her at the front door of her building with a curious, narrow-eyed gaze that stayed with her the rest of the day.

The phone on her desk rang early the following morning and she answered it absently while she typed.

"Do you still like symphony concerts?" came a deep voice in reply.

Alexander! Her fingers flew across the keys, making errors. "Uh, yes."

"There's a special performance of Debussy tomorrow night."

"I read about it in the entertainment section of the newspaper," she said. "They're doing 'Afternoon of a Faun' and 'La Mer,' my two favorites."

He chuckled. "I know."

"I'd love to see it," she admitted.

"I've got tickets. I'll pick you up at seven. Will you have time to eat supper by then?" he added, implying that he was asking her to the concert only, not to dinner.

"Of course," she replied.

"I have to work late, or I'd include dinner," he said softly.

"No problem, I have leftovers that have to be eaten," she said.

"Then I'll see you at seven."

"At seven." She hung up. Her hands were ice cold and shaking. She felt her insides shake. Alexander was taking her to a concert. Mentally her thoughts flew to her closet. She only had one good dress, a black one. She could pair it with her winter coat and a small strand of pearls that Margie and Alexander had given her when she graduated from college. She could put her hair up. She wouldn't look too bad.

She felt like a teenager on her first date until she realized why they were going out together. Alexander hadn't just discovered love eternal. He was putting on an act. But why put it on at a concert?

The answer came in an unexpected way. Brody stopped by her office a few minutes after Alexander's call. He came into the cubicle, looking nervous.

"Is something wrong?" she asked.

He drew in a long breath. "About next Saturday . . ." he began.

"I can't go," she blurted out.

His relief was patent. "I'm so glad you said that," he replied, relief making him limp. "Cara's going to be home and she wants to spend the day with me."

"Alexander's having a birthday party that day," she replied, painfully aware that she wouldn't be invited, although Alexander would surely want her co-workers to think that she was.

"I, uh, couldn't help but notice that he took you out to lunch yesterday," he said. "You've known him for a long time."

"A very long time," she confessed. "He just phoned, in fact, to invite me to a concert of Debussy . . ."

"Debussy?" he exclaimed.

"Well, yes . . . ?"

"I'll see you there," he said. "Cara and I are going, too. Isn't *that* a coincidence?"

She laughed, as he did. "I can't believe it! I didn't even know you liked Debussy!"

He grimaced. "Actually, I don't," he had to confess. "Cara does."

She smiled wickedly. "I don't think Alexander's very keen on him, either, but he'll pretend to be."

He smiled back. "Forgive me, but he doesn't seem quite your type," he began slowly, flushing a little. "He's a rather tough sort of man, isn't he? And I think he was wearing a gun yesterday, too . . . Jodie?" he added when she burst out laughing.

"He's sort of in security work, part-time,"

she told him, without adding where he worked or what he did. Alexander had always made a point of keeping his exact job secret, even among his friends, for reasons Jodie was only beginning to understand.

"Oh. Oh!" He laughed with sheer relief. "And here I thought maybe you were getting involved with a mobster!"

She'd have to remember to tell Alexander that. Not that it would impress him.

"No, he's not quite that bad," she assured him. "About next Saturday, Brody, I would have canceled anyway. It didn't feel right."

"No, it didn't," he seconded. "You and I are too conventional, Jodie. Neither of us is comfortable stepping out of bounds. I'll bet you never had a speeding ticket."

"Never," she agreed. "Not that I drive very much anymore. It's so convenient to take buses," she added, without mentioning that she'd had to sell her car months ago. The repair bills, because it was an older model, were eating her alive.

"I suppose so. Uh, I did notice that your friend drives a new Jaguar."

She smiled sedately. "He and his sister are independently wealthy," she told him. "They own a ranch and breed some of the finest cattle in south Texas. That's how he can afford to run a Jaguar."

"I see." He stuck his hands in his pockets and watched her. "Debussy. Somehow I never thought of you as a classical concert-goer."

"But I am. I love ballet and theater, too. Not that I get the opportunity to see much of them these days."

"Does your friend like them, too?"

"He's the one who taught me about them," she confided. "He was forever taking me and his sister to performances when we were in our teens. He said that we needed to learn culture, because it was important. We weren't keen at the time, but we learned to love it as he did. Except for Debussy," she added on a chuckle. "And I sometimes think I like that composer just to spite him."

"It's a beautiful piece, if you like modern. I'm a Beethoven man myself."

"And I don't like Beethoven, except for the Ninth Symphony."

"That figures. Well, thanks for understand-ing. I, uh, I guess we'll see you at the concert tonight, then!"

"I guess so."

They exchanged smiles and then he left. She turned her attention back to her com-puter, curious about the coincidence.

Had Alexander known that Brody and his

131

girlfriend Cara were going to the same performance? Or had it really been one of those inexplicable things?

Then another thought popped into her mind. What if Alexander was staking out her company because he suspected Brody of being in the drug lord's organization?

Six

The suspicion that Alexander was after Brody kept Jodie brooding for the rest of the day. Brody was a gentle, sweet man. Surely he couldn't be involved in anything as unsavory as drug smuggling!

If someone at the corporation was under investigation, she couldn't blow Alexander's cover by mentioning anything to her boss. But, wait, hadn't Alexander told his agent, Kennedy, that they were investigating a case at Thorn Oil Corporation? Then she remembered why Alexander wanted to pretend to be interested in Jodie. Something was crazy here. Why would he lie to Kennedy?

She shook her head and put the questions away. She wasn't going to find any answers on her own.

She'd been dressed and ready for an hour when she buzzed Alexander into her apartment building. By the time he got to her room and knocked at the door, she was a nervous wreck.

She opened the door, and he gave her a not very flattering scrutiny. She thought she looked nice in her sedate black dress and high heels, with her hair in a bun. Obviously he didn't. He was dashing, though, in a dinner jacket and slacks and highly polished black shoes. His black tie was perfectly straight against the expensive white cotton of his shirt.

"You never wear your hair down," Alexander said curtly. "And you've worn that same dress to two out of three parties at our house."

She flushed. "It's the only good dress I have, Alexander," she said tightly.

He sighed angrily. "Margie would love to make you something, if you'd let her."

She turned to lock her door. Her hands were cold and numb. He couldn't let her enjoy one single evening without criticizing something about her. She felt near tears . . .

She gasped as he suddenly whipped her around and bent to kiss her with grinding, passionate fervor. She didn't have time to respond. It was over as soon as it had begun, despite her rubbery legs and wispy breathing. She stood looking up at him with wide, misty, shocked eyes in a pale face.

His own green eyes glittered into hers as

he studied her reaction. "Stop letting me put you down," he said unexpectedly. "I know I don't do much for your ego, but you have to stand up for yourself. You're not a carpet, Jodie, stop letting people walk on you."

She was still trying to breathe and think at the same time.

"And now you look like an accident victim," he murmured. He pulled out a handkerchief, his eyes on her mouth. "I suppose I'm covered with pink lipstick," he added, pressing the handkerchief into her hand. "Clean me up."

"It . . . doesn't come off," she stammered.

He cocked an eyebrow and waited for an explanation.

"It's that new kind they advertise. You put it on and it lasts all day. It won't come off on coffee cups or even linen." She handed him back the handkerchief.

He put it up, but he didn't move. His hands went to the pert bun on the top of her head and before she could stop him, he loosed her hair from the circular comb that held the wealth of hair in place. It fell softly, in waves, to her shoulders.

Alexander caught his breath. "Beautiful," he whispered, the comb held absently in one hand while he ran the other through the soft strands of hair.

"It took forever . . . to get it put up," she protested weakly.

"I love long hair," he said gruffly. He bent, tilting her chin up, to kiss her with exquisite tenderness. "Leave it like that."

He put the comb in her hand and waited while she stuck it into her purse. Her hands shook. He saw that, too, and he smiled.

When she finished, he linked her fingers into his and they started off down the hall.

The concert hall was full. Apparently quite a few people in Houston liked Debussy, Jodie thought mischievously as they walked down the aisle to their seats. She knew that Alexander didn't like it at all, but it was nice of him to suffer through it, considering her own affection for the pieces the orchestra was playing.

Of course, he might only be here because he was spying on Brody, she thought, and then worried about that. She couldn't believe Brody would ever deal in anything dishonest. He was too much like Jodie herself. But why would Alexander be spending so much time at her place of work if he didn't suspect Brody?

It was all very puzzling. She sat down in the reserved seat next to Alexander and waited for the curtain to go up. They'd gotten into a traffic jam on the way and had arrived just in the nick of time. The lights went out almost the minute they sat down.

In the darkness, lit comfortably by the lights from the stage where the orchestra was placed, she felt Alexander's big, warm hand curl into hers. She sighed helplessly, loving the exciting, electric contact of his touch.

He heard the soft sound, and his fingers tightened. He didn't let go until intermission.

"Want to stretch your legs?" he invited, standing.

"Yes, I think so," she agreed. She got up, still excited by his proximity, and walked out with him. He didn't hold her hand this time, she noticed, and wondered why.

When they were in the lobby, Brody spotted them and moved quickly toward them, his girlfriend in tow.

She was pretty, Jodie noted, very elegant and dark-haired and long-legged. She wished she was half as pretty. Brody's girlfriend looked Hispanic. She was certainly striking.

"Well, hello!" Brody said with genuine warmth. "Sweetheart, this is my secretary, Jodie Clayburn . . . excuse me," he added quickly, with an embarrassed smile at Jodie's tightlipped glance, "I mean, my administrative assistant. And this is Jodie's date, Mr., uh, Mr. . . ."

"Cobb," Alexander prompted.

"Mr. Cobb," Brody parroted. "This is my girlfriend, Cara Dominguez," he introduced.

"Pleased to meet you," Cara said in a bored tone.

"Same here," Jodie replied.

"Cara's in marketing," Brody said, trying to force the conversation to ignite. "She works for Bradford Marketing Associates, down the street. They're a subsidiary of Ritter Oil Corporation. They sell drilling equipment and machine parts for oil equipment all over the United States. Cara is over the southwestern division."

"And what do you do, Mr. Cobb?" Cara asked Alexander, who was simply watching her, without commenting.

"Oh, he's in security work," Brody volunteered.

Cara's eyebrows arched. "Really!" she asked, but without much real interest.

"I work for the Drug Enforcement Administration," Alexander said with a faint smile, his eyes acknowledging Jodie's shock. "I'm undercover and out of the country a lot of the time," he added with the straightest face

Jodie had ever seen. "I don't have to work at all, of course," he added with a cool smile, "but I like the cachet of law enforcement duties."

Jodie was trying not to look at him or react. It was difficult.

"How nice," Cara said after a minute, and she seemed disconcerted by his honesty. "You are working on a case now?" she fished.

One of the first things Jodie and Margie had learned from Alexander when he went with the DEA was not to mention what he did for a living, past the fact that he did "security work." She'd always assumed it had something to do with his infrequent undercover assignments. And here he was spilling all the beans!

"Sort of," Alexander said lazily. "We're investigating a company with Houston connections," he added deliberately.

Cara was all ears. "That would not be Thorn Oil Corporation?"

Alexander gave her a very nice shocked look.

She laughed. "One hears things," she mused. "Don't worry, I never tell what I know."

"Right," Brody chuckled, making a joke of it. He hadn't known what Alexander did for a living until now.

Alexander laughed, too. "I have to have the occasional diversion," he confessed. "My father was wealthy. My sister and I were his only beneficiaries."

Cara was eyeing him with increased interest. "You live in Houston, Mr. Cobb?"

He nodded.

"Are you enjoying the concert?" Brody broke in, uncomfortable at the way his girlfriend was looking at Alexander.

"It's wonderful," Jodie said.

"I understand the Houston ballet is doing *The Nutcracker* starting in November," Cara purred, smiling at Alexander. "If you like ballet, perhaps we will meet again."

"Perhaps we will," Alexander replied. "Do you live in Houston, also, Miss Dominguez?"

"Yes, but I travel a great deal," she said with careless detachment. "My contacts are far reaching."

"She's only just come back from Mexico," Brody said with a nervous laugh.

"Yes, I've been helping my mother move," Cara said tightly. "After my father . . . died, she lost her home and had nowhere to go."

"I'm very sorry," Jodie told her. "I lost my parents some years ago. I know how it feels."

Cara turned back to Brody. "We need to

get back to our seats. Nice to have met you both," she added with a social smile as she took Brody's hand and drew him along with her. He barely had time to say goodbye.

Alexander glanced down at Jodie. "Your boss looked shocked when I told him what I did."

She shook her head. "You told me never to do that, but you told them everything!"

"I told them nothing Cara didn't know already," he said enigmatically. He slid his hand into hers and smiled secretively. "Let's go back."

"It's a very nice concert," she commented.

"Is it? I hate Debussy," he murmured unsurprisingly.

The comment kept her quiet until they were out of the theater and on their way back to her apartment in his car.

"Why did you ask me out if you don't like concerts?" she asked.

He glanced at her. "I had my reasons. What do you think of your boss's girlfriend?"

"She's nice enough. She leads Brody around like a child, though."

"Most women would," he said lazily. "He's not assertive."

"He certainly is," she defended him. "He has to fire people."

"He's not for you, Jodie, girlfriend or not," he said surprisingly. "You'd stagnate in a relationship with him."

"It's my life," she pointed out.

"So it is."

They went the rest of the way in silence. He walked her to her apartment door and stood staring down at her for a long moment. "Buy a new dress."

"Why?" she asked, surprised.

"I'll take you to see *The Nutcracker* next month. As I recall, it was one of your favorite ballets."

"Yes," she stammered.

"So I'll take you," he said. He checked his watch. "I've got a late call to make, and meetings the first of the week. But I'll take you to lunch next Wednesday."

"Okay," she replied.

He reached out suddenly and drew her against him, hard. He held her there, probing her eyes with his until her lips parted. Then he bent and kissed her hungrily, twisting his mouth against hers until she yielded and gave him what he wanted. A long, breathless moment later, he lifted his head.

"Not bad," he murmured softly. "But you could use a little practice. Sleep well."

He let her go and walked away while she tried to find her voice. He never looked back once. Jodie stood at her door watching until he stepped into the elevator and the doors closed.

She usually left at eleven-thirty to go to lunch, and Alexander knew it. But he was late the following Wednesday. She'd chewed off three of her long fingernails by the time he showed up. She was in the lobby where clients were met, along with several of her colleagues who were just leaving for lunch. Alexander came in, looking windblown and half out of humor.

"I can't make it for lunch," he said at once. "I'm sorry. Something came up."

"That's all right," she said, trying not to let her disappointment show. "Another time."

"I'll be out of town for the next couple of days," he continued, not lowering his voice, "but don't you forget my birthday party on Saturday. Call me from the airport and I'll pick you up. If I'm not back by then, Margie will. All right?"

Amazing how much he sounded as if he really wanted her to come. But she knew he was only putting on an act for the employees who were listening to him.

"All right," she agreed. "Have a safe trip. I'll see you Saturday."

He reached out and touched her cheek tenderly. "So long," he said, smiling. He walked away slowly, as if he hated to leave her, and she watched him go with equal reluctance. There were smiling faces all around. It was working. People believed they were involved, which was just what he wanted.

Later, while Brody was signing the letters he'd dictated earlier, she wondered where Alexander was going that would keep him out of town for so long.

"You look pensive," Brody said curiously. "Something worrying you?"

"Nothing, really," she lied. "I was just thinking about Alexander's birthday party on Saturday."

He sighed as he signed the last letter. "It must be nice to have a party," he murmured. "I stopped having them years ago."

"Cara could throw one for you," she suggested.

He grimaced. "She's not the least bit sentimental. She's all business, most of the time, and she never seems to stop working. She's on a trip to Arizona this week to try to land a new client."

"You'll miss her, I'm sure," Jodie said.

He shrugged. "I'll try to." He flushed. "Sorry, that just popped out."

She smiled. "We all have our problems, Brody."

"Yes, I noticed that your friend, Cobb, hardly touches you, except when he thinks someone is watching. He must be one cold fish," he added with disgust.

Jodie flushed then, remembering Alexander's ardor.

He cleared his throat and changed the subject, and not a minute too soon.

Jodie was doing housework in her apartment when the phone rang Saturday morning.

"Jodie?" Margie asked gently.

"Yes. How are you, Margie?" she asked, but not with her usual cheerful friendliness.

"You're still angry at me, aren't you?" She sighed. "I'm so sorry for making you do all the cooking . . ."

"I'm not angry," Jodie replied.

There was a long sigh. "I thought Kirry would help me arrange a showing of my designs at her department store," she confessed miserably. "But that's never going to happen. She only pretended to be my friend so that she could get to Alexander. I guess you know she's furious because he's been seen with you?"

"She has nothing to be jealous about,"

Jodie said coldly. "You can tell her so, for me. Was that all you wanted?"

"Jodie, that's not why I called!" Margie exclaimed. She hesitated. "Alexander wanted me to phone you and make sure you were coming to his birthday party."

"There's no chance of that," Jodie replied firmly.

"But . . . but he's expecting you," Margie stammered. "He said you promised to come, but that I had to call you and make sure you showed up."

"Kirry's invited, of course?" Jodie asked.

"Well . . . well, yes, I assumed he'd want her to come so I invited her, too."

"I'm invited to make her jealous, I suppose."

There was a static pause. "Jodie, what's going on? You won't return my calls, you won't meet me for lunch, you don't answer notes. If you're not mad at me, what's wrong?"

Jodie looked down at the floor. It needed mopping, she thought absently. "Alexander told you that he was sick of tripping over me every time he came back to the ranch, and that you were especially not to ask me to his birthday party."

There was a terrible stillness on the end of the line for several seconds. "Oh, my

146

God," Margie groaned. "You heard what he said that night!"

"I heard every single word, Margie," Jodie said tightly. "He thinks I'm still crazy about him, and it . . . disgusts him. He said I'm not in your social set and you should make friends among your own social circle." She took a deep, steadying breath. "Maybe he's right, Margie. The two of you took care of me when I had nobody else, but I've been taking advantage of it all these years, making believe that you were my family. In a way I'm grateful that Alexander opened my eyes. I've been an idiot."

"Jodie, he didn't mean it, I know he didn't! Sometimes he just says things without thinking them through. I know he wouldn't hurt you deliberately."

"He didn't know I could hear him," she said. "I drank too much and behaved like an idiot. We both know how Alexander feels about women who get drunk. But I've come to my senses now. I'm not going to impose on your hospitality . . ."

"But Alexander wants you to come!" Margie argued. "He said so!"

"No, he doesn't, Margie," Jodie said wistfully. "You don't understand what's going on, but I'm helping Alexander with a case. He's using me as a blind while he's surveilling a suspect, and don't you dare let on that you know it. It's not personal between us. It couldn't be. I'm not his sort of woman and we both know it."

Margie's intake of breath was audible. "What am I going to tell him when you don't show up?"

"You won't need to tell him anything," Jodie said easily. "He isn't expecting me. It was just for show. He'll tell you all about it one day. Now I have to go, Margie. I'm working in the kitchen, and things are going to burn," she added, lying through her teeth.

"We could have lunch next week," the other woman offered.

"No. You need to find friends in your class, Margie. I'm not part of your family, and you don't owe me anything. Now, goodbye!"

She hung up and unplugged the phone in case Margie tried to call back. She felt sick. But severing ties with Margie was the right thing to do. Once Alexander was through with her, once he'd caught his criminal, he'd leave her strictly alone. She was going to get out of his life, and Margie's, right now. It was the only sensible way to get over her feelings for Alexander.

The house was full of people when Alexander went inside, carrying his bag on a shoulder strap.

Margie met him at the door. "I'll bet you're tired, but at least you got here." She chuckled, trying not to show her worry. "Leave your bag by the door and come on in. Everybody's in the dining room with the cake."

He walked beside her toward the spacious dining room, where about twenty people were waiting near a table set with china and crystal, punch and coffee and cake. He searched the crowd and began to scowl.

"I don't see Jodie," he said at once. "Where is she? Didn't you phone her?"

"Yes," she groaned, "but she wouldn't come. Please, Lex, can't we talk about it later? Look, Kirry's here!"

"Damn Kirry," he said through his teeth, glaring down at his sister. "Why didn't she come?"

She drew in a miserable breath. "Because she heard us talking the last time she was here," she replied slowly. "She said you were right about her not being in our social class, and that she heard you say that the last thing you wanted was to trip over her at your birthday party." She winced, because the look on his face was so full of pain.

"She heard me," he said, almost choking

on the words. "Good God, no wonder she looked at me the way she did. No wonder she's been acting so strangely!"

"She won't go out to lunch with me, she won't come here, she doesn't even want me to call her anymore," Margie said sadly. "I feel as if I've lost my own sister."

His own loss was much worse. He felt sick to his soul. He'd never meant for Jodie to hear those harsh, terrible words. He'd been reacting to his own helpless loss of control with her, not her hesitant ardor. It was himself he'd been angry at. Now he understood why Jodie was so reluctant to be around him lately. It was ironic that he found himself thinking about her around the clock, and she was as standoffish as a woman who found him bad company when they were alone. If only he could turn the clock back, make everything right. Jodie, so sweet and tender and loving, Jodie who had loved him once, hearing him tell Margie that Jodie disgusted him . . . !

"I should be shot," he ground out. "Shot!"

"Don't. It's your birthday," Margie reminded him. "Please. All these people came just to wish you well."

He didn't say another word. He simply walked into the room and let the congratulations flow over him. But he didn't feel happy. He felt as if his heart had withered and died in his chest.

That night, he slipped into his office while Kirry was talking to Margie, and he phoned Jodie. He'd had two straight malt whiskeys with no water, and he wasn't quite sober. It had taken that much to dull the sharp edge of pain.

"You didn't come," he said when she answered.

She hadn't expected him to notice. She swallowed, hard. "The invitation was all for show," she said, her voice husky. "You didn't expect me."

There was a pause. "Did you go out with Brody after all?" he drawled sarcastically. "Is that why you didn't show up?"

"No, I didn't," she muttered. "I'm not spending another minute of my life trying to fit into your exalted social class," she added hotly. "Cheating wives, consciousless husbands, social climbing friends . . . that's not my idea of a party!"

He sat back in his chair. "You might not believe it, but it's not mine, either," he said flatly. "I'd rather get a fast food hamburger and talk shop with the guys."

That was surprising. But she didn't quite trust him. "That isn't Kirry's style," she pointed out.

He laughed coldly. "It would become her style in minutes if she thought it would make me propose. I'm rich. Haven't you noticed?"

"It's hard to miss," she replied.

"Kirry likes life in the fast lane. She wants to be decked out in diamonds and taken to all the most expensive places four nights a week. Five on holidays."

"I'm sure she wants you, too."

"Are you?"

"I'm folding clothes, Alexander. Was there anything else?" she added formally, trying to get him to hang up. The conversation was getting painful.

"I never knew that you heard me the night of our last party, Jodie," he said in a deep, husky, pained sort of voice. "I'm more sorry than I can say. You don't know what it was like when my mother had parties. She drank like a fish . . ."

So Margie had told him. It wasn't really a surprise. "I had some champagne," she interrupted. "I don't drink, so it overwhelmed me. I'm very sorry for the way I behaved."

There was another pause. "I loved it," he said gruffly.

Now she couldn't even manage a reply. She just stared at the receiver, waiting for

152

him to say something else.

"Talk to me!" he growled.

"What do you want me to say?" she asked unsteadily. "You were right. I don't belong in your class. I never will. You said I was a nuisance, and you were ri—"

"Jodie!" Her name sounded as if it were torn from his throat. "Jodie, don't! I didn't mean what I said. You've never been a nuisance!"

"It's too late," she said heavily. "I won't come back to the ranch again, ever, Alexander, not for you or even for Margie. I'm going to live my own life, make my own way in the world."

"By pushing us out of it?" he queried.

She sighed. "I suppose so."

"But not until I solve this case," he added after a minute. "Right?"

She wanted to argue, but she kept seeing the little boys' faces in that photograph he'd shown her. "Not until then," she said.

There was a rough sound, as if he'd been holding his breath and suddenly let it out. "All right."

"Alexander, where are you?!" That was Kirry's voice, very loud.

"In a minute, Kirry! I'm on the phone!"

"We're going to open the presents. Come on!"

Jodie heard the sound Alexander made, and she laughed softly in spite of herself. "I thought it was your birthday?" she mused.

"It started to be, but my best present is back in Houston folding clothes," he said vehemently.

Her heart jumped. She had to fight not to react. "I'm nobody's present, Alexander," she informed him. "And now I really do have to go. Happy birthday."

"I'm thirty-four," he said. "Margie is the only family I have. Two of my colleagues just had babies," he remarked, his voice just slightly slurred. "Their desks are full of photographs of the kids and their wives. Know what I've got in a frame on my desk, Jodie? Kirry, in a ball gown."

"I guess the married guys would switch places with you . . ."

"That's not what I mean! I didn't put it there, she did. Instead of a wife and kids, I've got a would-be debutante who wants to own Paris."

"That was your choice," she pointed out.

"That's what you think. She gave me the framed picture." There was a pause. "Why don't you give me a photo?"

"Sure. Why not? Who would you like a photo of, and I'll see if I can find one for you."

"You, idiot!"

"I don't have any photos of myself."

"Why not?"

"Who'd take them?" she asked. "I don't even own a camera."

"We'll have to do something about that," he murmured. "Do you like parks? We could go jogging early Monday in that one near where you live. The one with the goofy sculpture."

"It's modern art. It isn't goofy."

"You're entitled to your opinion. Do you jog?"

"Not really."

"Do you have sweats and sneakers?"

She sighed irritably. "Well, yes, but . . ."

"No buts. I'll see you bright and early Monday." There was a pause. "I'll even apologize."

"That would be a media event."

"I'm serious," he added quietly. "I've never regretted anything in my life more than knowing you heard what I said to Margie that night."

For an apology, it was fairly headlong. Alexander never made apologies. It was a red letter event.

'Okay," she said after a few seconds.

He sighed, hard. "We can start over," he said firmly.

"Alexander, are you coming out of there?" came Kirry's petulant voice in the background.

"Better tell Kirry first," she chided.

"I'll tell her . . . get the hell out of my study!" he raged abruptly, and there was the sound of something heavy hitting the wall. Then there was the sound of a door closing with a quick snap.

"What did you do?" Jodie exclaimed.

"I threw a book in her general direction. Don't worry. It wasn't a book I liked. It was something on Colombian politics."

"You could have hit her!"

"In pistol competition, I hit one hundred targets out of a hundred shots. The book hit ten feet from where she was standing."

"You shouldn't throw things at people."

"But I'm uncivilized," he reminded her. "I need someone to mellow me out."

"Kirry's already there."

"Not for long, if she opens that damned door again. I'll see you Monday. Okay?"

There was a long hesitation. But finally she said, "Okay."

She put down the receiver and stared at it blankly. Her life had just shifted ten degrees and she had no idea why. At least, not right then.

SEVEN

Jodie had just changed into her sweats and was making breakfast in her sock feet when Alexander knocked on the door.

He was wearing gray sweats, like hers, with gray running shoes. He gave her a long, thorough appraisal. "I don't like your hair in a bun," he commented.

"I can't run with it down," she told him. "It tangles."

He sniffed the air. "Breakfast?" he asked hopefully.

"Just bacon and eggs and biscuits."

"Just! I had a granola bar," he said with absolute disdain.

She laughed nervously. It was new to have him in her apartment, to have him wanting to be with her. She didn't understand his change of attitude, and she didn't really trust it. But she was too enchanted to question it too closely.

"If you'll feed me," he began, "I'll let you

keep up with me while we jog."

"That sounds suspiciously like a bribe," she teased, moving toward the table. "What *would* your bosses say?"

"You're not a client," he pointed out, seating himself at the table. "Or a perpetrator. So it doesn't count."

She poured him a mug of coffee and put it next to his plate, frowning as she noted the lack of matching dishes and even silverware. The table — a prize from a yard sale — had noticeable scratches and she didn't even have a tablecloth.

"What a comedown this must be," she muttered to herself as she fetched the blackberry jam and put it on the table, along with another teaspoon that didn't match the forks.

He gave her an odd look. "I'm not making comparisons, Jodie," he said softly, and his eyes were as soft as his deep voice. "You live within your means, and you do extremely well at it. You'd be surprised how many people are mortgaged right down to the fillings in their teeth trying to put on a show for their acquaintances. Which is, incidentally, why a lot of them end up in prison, trying to make a quick buck by selling drugs."

She made a face. "I'd rather starve than

live like that."

"So would I," he confessed. He bit into a biscuit and moaned softly. "If only Jessie could make these the way you do," he said.

She smiled, pleased at the compliment, because Jessie was a wonderful cook. "They're the only thing I do well."

"No, they aren't." He tasted the jam and frowned. "I didn't know they made black-berry jam," he noted.

"You can buy it, but I like to make my own and put it up," she said. "That came from blackberries I picked last summer, on the ranch. They're actually your own black-berries," she added sheepishly.

"You can have as many as you like, if you'll keep me supplied with this jam," he said, helping himself to more biscuits.

"I'm glad you like it."

They ate in a companionable silence. When she poured their second cups of strong coffee, there weren't any biscuits left.

"Now I need to jog," he teased, "to work off the weight I've just put on. Coffee's good, too, Jodie. Everything was good."

"You were just hungry."

He sat back holding his coffee and stared at her. "You've never learned how to take a compliment," he said gently. "You do a lot of things better than other people, but you're modest to the point of self-abasement."

She moved a shoulder. "I like cooking."

He sipped coffee, still watching her. She was pretty early in the morning, he mused, with her face blooming like a rose, her skin clean and free of makeup. Her lips had a natural blush, and they had a shape that was arousing. He remembered how it felt to kiss her, and he ached to do it again. But this was new territory for her. He had to take his time. If he rushed her, he was going to lose her. That thought, once indifferent, took on supreme importance now. He was only beginning to see how much a part of him Jodie already was. He could have kicked himself for what he'd said to her at the ill-fated party.

"The party was a bust," he said abruptly.

Her eyes widened. "Pardon?"

"Kirry opened the presents and commented on their value and usefulness until the guests turned to strong drink," he said with a twinkle in his green eyes. "Then she took offense when a former friend of hers turned up with her ex-boyfriend and made a scene. She left in a trail of flames by cab before we even got to the live band."

She was trying not to smile. It was hard not to be amused at Kirry's situation. The woman was trying, even to people like Margie, who wanted to be friends with her.

"I guess there went Margie's shot at fashion fame," she said sadly.

"Kirry would never have helped her," he said carelessly, and finished his coffee. "She never had any intention of risking her job on a new designer's reputation. She was stringing Margie along so that she could hang out with us. She was wearing thin even before Saturday night."

"Sorry," she said, not knowing what else to say.

"We weren't lovers," he offered blatantly.

She blushed and then caught her breath. "Alexander . . . !"

"I wanted you to know that, in case anything is ever said about my relationship with her," he added, very seriously. "It was never more than a surface attraction. I can't abide a woman who wears makeup to bed."

She wouldn't ask, she wouldn't ask, she wouldn't . . . ! "How do you know she does?" she blurted out.

He grinned at her. "Margie told me. She asked Kirry why, and Kirry said you never knew when a gentleman might knock on your door after midnight." He leaned forward. "I never did."

"I wasn't going to ask!"

"Sure you were." His eyes slid over her pretty breasts, nicely but not blatantly outlined under the gray jersey top she was wearing. "You're possessive about me. You don't want to be, but you are."

She was losing ground. She got to her feet and made a big thing of checking to see that her shoelaces were tied. "Shouldn't we go?"

He got up, stretched lazily, and started to clear the table. She was shocked to watch him.

"You've never done that," she remarked.

He glanced at her. "If I get married, and I might, I think marriage should be a fifty-fifty proposition. There's nothing romantic about a man lying around the apartment in a dirty T-shirt watching football while his wife slaves in the kitchen." He frowned thoughtfully. "Come to think of it, I don't like football."

"You don't wear dirty T-shirts, either," she replied, feeling sad because he'd mentioned marrying. Maybe there was another woman in his life, besides Kirry.

He chuckled. "Not unless I'm working in the garage." He came around the table after he'd put the dishes in the sink and took her gently by the shoulders, his expression somber. "We've never discussed personal issues. I know less about you than a stranger does. Do you like children? Do you want to have them? Or is a career primary in your life right now?"

The questions were vaguely terrifying. He was going from total indifference to intent scrutiny, and it was too soon. Her face took on a hunted look.

"Never mind," he said quickly, when he saw that. "Don't worry about the question. It isn't important."

She relaxed, but only a little. "I . . . love children," she faltered. "I like working, or I would if I had a challenging job. But that doesn't mean I'd want to put off having a family if I got married. My mother worked while I was growing up, but she was always there when I needed her, and she never put her job before her family. Neither would I." She searched his eyes, thinking how beautiful a shade of green they were, and about little children with them. Her expression went dreamy. "Fame and fortune may sound enticing, but they wouldn't make up for having people love you." She shrugged. "I guess that sounds corny."

"Actually, it sounds very mature." He bent and drew his mouth gently over her lips, a whisper of contact that didn't demand anything. "I feel the same way."

"You do?" She was unconsciously reaching up to him, trying to prolong the contact. It was unsettling that his lightest touch could send her reeling like this. She wanted more. She wanted him to crush her in his arms and kiss her blind.

He nibbled her upper lip slowly. "It isn't enough, is it?"

"Well . . . no . . ."

His arms drew her up, against the steely length of his body, and his mouth opened her lips to a kiss that was consuming with its heat. She moaned helplessly, clinging to him.

He lifted his mouth a breath away. His voice was strained when he spoke. "Do you have any idea what those little noises do to me?" he groaned.

"Noises?" she asked, oblivious, as she stared at his mouth.

"Never mind." He kissed her again, devouring her soft lips. The sounds she made drugged him. He was measuring the distance from the kitchen to her bedroom when he realized how fast things were progressing.

He drew back, and held her away from him, his jaw taut with an attempt at control.

"Alexander," she whispered, her voice pleading as she looked up at him with misty soft eyes.

"I almost never get women pregnant on Monday, but this could be an exception," he said in a choked tone.

Her eyes widened like saucers as she realized what he was saying.

He burst out laughing at her expression. He moved back even more. "I only carry identification and twenty dollars on me when I jog," he confessed. "The other things I keep in my wallet are still in it, at my apartment," he added, his tone blatantly expressive.

She divined what he was intimating and she flushed. She pushed back straggly hair from her face as she searched for her composure.

"Of course, a lot of modern women keep their own supply," he drawled. "I expect you have a box full in your medicine cabinet."

She flushed even more, and now she was glaring at him.

He chuckled, amused. "Your parents were very strict," he recalled. "And deeply religious. You still have those old attitudes about premarital sex, don't you?"

She nodded, grimacing.

"Don't apologize," he said wistfully. "In ten minutes or so, the ache will ease and I can actually stand up straight . . . God, Jodie!" he burst out laughing at her horrified expression. "I'm kidding!"

"You're a terrible man," she moaned.

"No, I'm just normal," he replied. "I'd love nothing better than a few hours in bed with you, but I'm not enough of a scoundrel to seduce you. Besides all that —" he sighed "— your conscience would kill both of us."

"Rub it in."

He shrugged. "You'd be surprised how many women at my office abstain, and make no bones about it to eligible bachelors who want to take them out," he said, and he smiled tenderly at her. "We tend to think of them as rugged individualists with the good sense not to take chances." He leaned forward. "And there are actually a couple of the younger male agents who feel the same way!"

"You're kidding!"

He shook his head, smiling. "Maybe it's a trend. You know, back in the early twentieth century, most women and men went to their weddings chaste. A man with a bad reputation was as untouchable as a woman with one."

"I'll bet you never told a woman in your life that you were going to abstain," she murmured wickedly.

He didn't smile back. He studied her for a long moment. "I'm telling you that I am.

For the foreseeable future."

She didn't know how to take that, and it showed.

"I'm not in your class as a novice," he confessed, "but I'm no rake, either. I don't find other women desirable lately. Just you." He shrugged. "Careful, it may be contagious."

She laughed. Her whole face lit up. She was beautiful.

He drew her against him and kissed her, very briefly, before he moved away again. "We should go," he said. "I have a meeting at the office at ten. Then we could have lunch."

"Okay," she said. She felt lighthearted. Overwhelmed. She started toward the door and then stopped. "Can I ask you a question?"

"Shoot."

"Are you staking out my company because you're investigating Brody for drug smuggling?"

He gave her an old, wise look. "You're sharp, Jodie. I'll have to watch what I say around you."

"That means you're not going to tell me. Right?"

He chuckled. "Right." He led the way into the hall and then waited for her to lock her door behind them.

She slipped the key into her pocket.

"No ID?" he mused as they went downstairs and started jogging down the sparsely occupied sidewalk.

"Just the key and five dollars, in case I need money for a bottle of water or something," she confessed.

He sighed, not even showing the strain as they moved quickly along. "One of our forensic reconstruction artists is always lecturing us on carrying identification. She says that it's easier to have something on you that will identify you, so that she doesn't have to take your skull and model clay to do a reconstruction of your face. She helps solve a lot of murder victims' identities, but she has plenty that she can't identify. The faces haunt her, she says."

"I watched a program about forensic reconstruction on educational television two weeks ago."

"I know the one you mean. I saw it, too. That was our artist," he said with traces of pride in his deep voice. "She's a wonder."

"I guess it wouldn't hurt to carry my driver's license around with me," she murmured.

He didn't say another word, but he grinned to himself.

■ ■ ■ ■

The meeting was a drug task force formed of a special agent from the Houston FBI office, a Houston police detective who specialized in local gangs, a Texas Ranger from Company A, an agent from the U.S. Customs Service and a sheriff's deputy from Harris County who headed her department's drug unit.

They sat down in a conference room in the nearest Houston police station to discuss intelligence.

"We've got a good lead on the new division chief of the Culebra cartel in Mexico," Alexander announced when it was his turn to speak. "We know that he has somebody on his payroll from Ritter Oil Corporation, and that he's funneling drugs through a warehouse where oil regulators and drilling equipment are kept before they're shipped out all over the southwest. Since the parking lot of that warehouse is locked by a key code, the division chief has to have someone on the inside."

"Do we know how it's being moved and when?" the FBI agent asked.

Alexander had suspicions, but no concrete evidence. "Waiting for final word on when.

But we do have an informant, a young man who got cold feet and came to U.S. Customs with information about the drug smuggling. I interviewed the young man, with help from customs," he added, nodding with a smile at the petite brunette customs official at the table with them.

"That would be me," she said with a grin.

"The informant says that a shipment of processed cocaine is on the way here, one of the biggest in several years. It was shipped from the Guajira Peninsula in Colombia to Central America and transshipped by plane to an isolated landing site in rural Mexico. From there it was carried to a warehouse in Mexico City owned by a subsidiary of an oil company here in Houston. It was reboxed with legitimate oil processing equipment manufactured in Europe, in boxes with false bottoms. It was shipped legally to the oil company's district office in Galveston where it was inspected briefly and passed through customs."

"The oil company is one that's never been involved in any illegal activity," the customs representative said wistfully, "so the agent didn't look for hidden contraband."

"To continue," Alexander said, "it's going to be shipped into the Houston warehouse via the Houston Ship Canal as domestic inventory from Galveston."

"Which means, no more customs inspections," the Texas Ranger said.

"Exactly," Alexander agreed.

The brunette customs agent shook her head. "A few shipments get by our inspectors, but not many. We have contacts everywhere, too, and one of those tipped us off about the young man who was willing to inform on the perpetrators of an incoming cocaine shipment," she told the others. "So we saved our bacon."

"You had the contacts I gave you, don't forget," the blond lieutenant of detectives from Houston reminded her with a smile, as she adjusted her collar.

"Do we even have a suspect?" the customs agent asked.

Alexander nodded. "I've got someone on the inside at Ritter Oil, and I'm watching a potential suspect. I don't have enough evidence yet to make an accusation, but I hope to get it, and soon. I'm doing this undercover, so this information is to be kept in this room. I've put it out that we have another company, Thorn Oil, under surveillance, as a cover story. Under no circumstances are any of you to discuss any of this meeting, even with another DEA agent — *especially* with another DEA agent — until further notice. That's essential."

The police lieutenant gave him a pointed look. "Can I ask why?"

"Because the oil corporation isn't the only entity that's harboring an inside informant," Alexander replied flatly. "And that's all I feel comfortable saying."

"You can count on us," the Texas Ranger assured him. "We won't blow your cover. The person you're watching, can you tell us why you're watching him?"

"In order to use that warehouse for storage purposes, the drug lord has to have access to it," Alexander explained. "I'm betting he has some sort of access to the locked gate and that he's paying the night watchman to look the other way."

"That would make sense," the customs agent agreed grimly. "These people know how little law enforcement personnel make. They can easily afford to offer a poorly paid night watchman a six figure 'donation' to just turn his head at the appropriate time."

"That much money would tempt even a law-abiding citizen," Alexander agreed. "But more than that, very often there's a need that compromises integrity. A sheriff in another state had a wife dying of cancer and no insurance. He got fifty thousand dollars for not noticing a shipment of drugs coming into his county."

"They catch him?" the policewoman asked.

"Yes. He wasn't very good at being a crook. He confessed, before he was even suspected of being involved."

"How many people in your agency know about this?" the deputy sheriff asked Alexander.

"Nobody, at the moment," he replied. "It has to stay that way, until we make the bust. I'll depend on all of you to back me up. The mules working for the new drug lord carry automatic weapons and they've killed so many people down in Mexico that they won't hesitate to waste anyone who gets in their way."

"Good thing the president of Mexico isn't intimidated by them," the customs agent said with a grin. "He's done more to attack drug trafficking than any president before him."

"He's a good egg," Alexander agreed. "Let's hope we can shut down this operation before any more kids go down."

"Amen to that," the FBI agent said solemnly.

Alexander showed up at Jodie's office feeling more optimistic than he had for weeks.

He was close to an arrest, but the next few days would be critical. After their meeting, the task force had gleaned information from the informant that the drug shipment was coming into Houston the following week. He had to be alert, and he had to spend a lot of time at Jodie's office so that he didn't miss anything.

He took her out to lunch, but he was preoccupied.

"You're onto something," she guessed.

He nodded, smiling. "Something big. How would you like to be part of a surveillance?"

"Me? Wow. Can I have a gun?"

He glared at her. "No."

She shrugged. "Okay. But don't expect me to save your life without one."

"Not giving you one might save my life," he said pointedly.

She ignored the jibe. "Surveillance?" she prodded. "Of what?"

"You'll find out when we go, and not a word to anybody."

"Okay," she agreed. "How do you do surveillance?"

"We sit in a parked car and drink coffee and wish we were watching television," he said honestly. "It gets incredibly boring. Not so much if we have a companion. That's where you come in," he added with a grin.

"We can sit in the car and neck and nobody will guess we're spying on them."

"In a Jaguar," she murmured. "Sure, nobody will notice us in one of those!"

He gave her a long look. "We'll be in a law enforcement vehicle, undercover."

"Right. In a car with government license plates, four antennae and those little round hubcaps . . ."

"Will you stop?" he groaned.

"Sorry!" She grinned at him over her coffee. "But I like the necking part."

He pursed his lips and gave her a wicked grin. "So do I."

She laughed a little self-consciously and finished her lunch.

They were on the way back to his Jaguar when his DEA agent, Kennedy, drove up. He got out of his car and approached them with a big smile.

"Hi, Cobb! How's it going?" he asked.

"Couldn't be better," Alexander told him complacently. "What's new?"

"Oh, nothing, I'm still working on that smuggling ring." He glanced at Alexander curiously. "Heard anything about a new drug task force?"

"Just rumors," Alexander assured him, and noticed a faint reaction from the other man. "Nothing definite. I'll let you know if

I hear anything."

"Thanks." Kennedy shrugged. "There are always rumors."

"Do you have anybody at Thorn Oil, just in case?" Alexander asked him pointedly.

Kennedy cleared his throat and laughed. "Nobody at all. Why?"

"No reason. No reason at all. Enjoy your lunch."

"Sure. I never see you at staff meetings lately," he added. "You got something undercover going on?"

Alexander deliberately tugged Jodie close against his side and gave her a look that could have warmed coffee. "Something," he said, with a smile in Kennedy's direction. "See you."

"Yeah. See you!"

Kennedy walked on toward the restaurant, a little distracted.

Jodie waited until they were closed up in Alexander's car before she spoke. "You didn't tell him anything truthful," she remarked.

"Kennedy's got a loose tongue," he told her as he cranked the car. "You don't tell him anything you don't want repeated. Honest to God, he's worse than Margie!"

"So that's it," she said, laughing. "I just wondered. Isn't it odd that he seems to show up at places where we eat a lot?"

"Plenty of the guys eat where we do," he replied lazily. "We know where the good food is."

"You really do," she had to admit. "That steak was wonderful!"

"Glad you liked it."

"I could cook for you, sometime," she offered, and then flushed at her own boldness.

"After I wind up this case, I'll let you," he said, with a warm smile. "Meanwhile, I've got a lot of work to do."

She wondered about that statement after he left her at the office. She was still puzzling over it when she walked right into Brody when she got off the elevator at her floor.

"Oh, sorry!" she exclaimed, only then noticing that Cara was with him. "Hello," she greeted the woman as she stopped to punch her time card before entering the cubicle area.

Cara wasn't inclined to be polite. She gave Jodie a cold look and turned back to Brody. "I don't understand why you can't do me this one little favor," she muttered. "It isn't as if I ask you often for anything."

"Yes, but dear, it's an odd place to leave your car. There are garages . . ."

"My car is very expensive," she pointed out, her faint accent growing in intensity, like the anger in her black eyes. "All I require is for you to let me in, only that."

Jodie's ears perked up. She pretended to have trouble getting her card into the time clock, and hummed deliberately to herself, although not so loudly that she couldn't hear what the other two people were saying.

"Company rules . . ." he began.

"Rules, rules! You are to be an executive, are you not? Do you have to ask permission for such a small thing? Or are you not man enough to make such decisions for yourself?" she added cannily.

"Nice to see you both," Jodie said, and moved away — but not quickly. She fumbled in her purse and walked very slowly as she did. She was curious to know what Cara wanted.

"I suppose I could, just this once," Brody capitulated. "But you know, dear, a warehouse isn't as safe as a parking garage, strictly speaking."

Jodie's heart leaped.

"Yours certainly is, you have an armed guard, do you not? Besides, I work for a subsidiary of Ritter Oil. It is not as if I had no right to leave my car there when I go out of town for the company."

"All right, all right," Brody said. "Tomorrow night then. What time?"

"At six-thirty," she told him. "It will be dark, so you must flash your lights twice to let me know it is you."

They spoke at length, but Jodie was already out of earshot. She'd heard enough of the suspicious conversation to wonder about it. But she was much too cautious to phone Alexander from her work station.

She would have to wait until the end of the day, even if it drove her crazy. Meanwhile she pretended that she'd noticed nothing.

Brody came by her cubicle later that afternoon, just before quitting time, while she was finishing a letter he'd dictated.

"Can I help you?" she asked automatically, and smiled.

He smiled back and looked uncomfortable. "No, not really. I just wondered what you thought about what Cara asked me?"

She gave him a blank look. "What she asked you?" she said. "I'm sorry, I'd just come from having lunch with Alexander." She smiled and sighed and lowered her eyes demurely. "To tell you the truth, I wasn't paying attention to anything except the time clock. What did she ask you?" She opened her eyes very wide and looked blank.

"Never mind. She phoned and made a comment about your being there. It's nothing. Nothing at all."

She smiled up at him. "Did you enjoy the concert that night?"

"Yes, actually I did, despite the fact that Cara went out to the powder room and didn't show up again for an hour." He shook his head. "Honestly, that woman is so mysterious! I never know what she's thinking."

"She's very crisp, isn't she?" she mused. "I mean, she's assertive and aggressive. I guess she's a good marketer."

"She is," he sighed. "At least, I guess she is. I haven't heard much from the big boss about her work. In fact, there was some talk about letting her go a month or two ago, because she lost a contract. Funny, it was one she was supposedly out of town negotiating at the time, but the client said he'd never seen her. Mr. Ritter talked him into staying, but he had words with Cara about the affair."

"Could that have been when her mother was ill?" she asked.

"Her mother hasn't ever been ill, as far as I know," he murmured. "She did move from Peru to Mexico, but you know about that." He put his hands in his pockets. "She wants me to do something that isn't quite acceptable, and I'm nervous about it. I'm due for a promotion. I don't want to get mixed up in anything the least bit suspicious."

"Why, Brody, what does she want you to do?" she asked innocently.

He glanced at her, started to speak, and then smiled sheepishly. "Well, it's nothing, really. Just a favor." He shrugged. "I'm sure I'm making a big deal out of nothing. You never told me that your boyfriend works for the Drug Enforcement Administration."

"He doesn't advertise it," she stammered. "He does a lot of undercover work at night," she added.

Brody sighed. "I see. Well, I'll let you finish. You and Cobb seem to get along very well," he added.

"I've known him a long time."

"So you have. You've known me a long time, too, though," he added with a slow smile.

"Not really. Only three years."

"Is it? I thought it was longer." He toyed with his tie. "You and Cobb seem to spend a lot of time together."

"Not as much as we'd like," she said, seeing a chance to help Alexander and throw Cara off the track. "And I have a cousin staying with me for a few days, so we spend a lot of time in parked cars necking," she added.

Brody actually flushed. "Oh." He glanced at his watch and grimaced. "I've got a meeting with our vice president in charge of human resources at four, I'd better get going. See you later."

"See you, Brody."

She was very glad that she'd learned to keep what she knew to herself. What Brody's girlfriend had let slip was potentially explosive information, even if it was only circumstantial. She'd have a lot to tell Alexander when she saw him. Furthermore, she'd already given Alexander some cover by telling Brody about the company car, and the fact that they spent time at night necking in one. He was going to be proud of her, she just knew it!

EIGHT

The minute she got to her apartment, Jodie grabbed the phone and called Alexander.

"Can you come by right away?" Jodie asked him quickly.

He hesitated. "To your apartment? Why?"

She didn't know if her phone might be bugged. She couldn't risk it. She sighed theatrically. "Because I'm wearing a see-through gown with a row of prophylactics pinned to the hem . . . !"

"Jodie!" He sounded shocked.

"Listen, I have something to tell you," she said firmly.

He hesitated again and then he groaned. "I can't right now . . ."

"Who's on the phone, Alex?" came a sultry voice from somewhere in the background.

Jodie didn't need to ask who the voice belonged to. Her heart began to race with impotent fury. "Sorry I interrupted," she said flatly. "I'm sure you and Kirry have lots to talk about."

She hung up and then unplugged the phone. So much for any feeling Alexander had for her. He was already seeing Kirry again, alone and at his apartment. No doubt he was only seeing Jodie to avert suspicion at Ritter Oil. The sweet talk was to allay any suspicion that he was using her. Why hadn't she realized that? The Cobbs were always using her, for one reason or another. She was being a fool again. Despite what he'd said, it was obvious now that Alexander had no interest in her except as a pawn.

She fought down tears and went to her computer. She might as well use some of her expertise to check out Miss Cara Dominguez and see if the woman had a rap sheet. With a silent apology to the local law enforcement departments, she hacked into criminal files and checked her out.

What she found was interesting enough to take her mind off Alexander. It seemed that Cara didn't have a lily-white past at all. In fact, she'd once been arrested for possession with intent to distribute cocaine and had managed to get the charges dropped. Besides that, she had some very odd connections internationally. It was hinted in the records of an international law enforcement agency — whose files gave way to her expertise also — that her uncle was one of the Colombian drug lords. She wondered if Alexander knew that.

Would he care? He was with Kirry. Damn Kirry! She threw a plastic coffee cup at the wall in impotent rage.

Just as it hit, there was a buzz at the intercom. She glowered at it, but the caller was insistent. She pushed the button.

"Yes?" she asked angrily.

"Let me in," Alexander said tersely.

"Are you alone?" she asked with barely contained sarcasm.

"In more ways than you might realize," he replied, his voice deep and subdued. "Let me in, Jodie."

She buzzed him in with helpless reluctance and waited at her opened door for him to come out of the elevator.

He was still in his suit. He looked elegant, expensive, and very irritated. He walked into the apartment ahead of her and went straight to the kitchen.

"I was going to take you out to eat when Kirry showed up, in tears, and begged to talk to me," he said heavily, examining pots until he found one that contained a nice beef stew. He got a bowl out of the cupboard and proceeded to fill it. "Any corn bread?"

he asked wistfully, having sniffed it when he entered the apartment.

"It's only just getting done," she said, reaching around him for a pot holder. She opened the oven and produced a pone of corn bread.

"I'm hungry," he said.

"You're always hungry," she accused, but she was feeling better.

He caught her by the shoulders and pulled her against him, tilting her chin up so that he could see into her mutinous eyes. "I don't want Kirry. I said that, and I meant it."

"Even if you did, you couldn't say so," she muttered. "You need me to help you smoke out your drug smuggler."

He scowled. "Do you really think I'm that sort of man?" he asked, and sounded wounded. "I'll admit that Margie and I don't have a good track record with you, but I'd draw the line at pretending an emotion I didn't feel, just to catch crooks."

She shifted restlessly and didn't speak.

He shook his head. "No ego," he mused, watching her. "None at all. You can't see what's right under your nose."

"My chin, and no, I can't see it . . ."

He chuckled, bending to kiss her briefly, fiercely. "Feed me. Then we might watch television together for a while. I'll be working most evenings during the week, but Friday night we could go see a movie or something."

Her heart skipped. "A movie?"

"Or we could go bowling. I used to like it."

Her mind was spinning. He actually wanted to be with her! But cold reality worked its way between them again. "You haven't asked why I wanted you to come over," she began as he started for the table with his bowl of stew.

"No, I haven't. Why?" he asked, pouring himself a cup of freshly brewed coffee and accepting a dish of corn bread from her.

She put coffee and corn bread at her place at the table and put butter next to it before she sat down and gave Alexander a mischievous smile. "Cara talked Brody into letting her into the warehouse parking lot after hours tomorrow — about six-thirty in the evening. She said she wanted to park her car there, but it sounded thin to me."

He caught his breath. "Jodie, you're a wonder."

"That's not all," she added, sipping coffee and adding more cream to it. "She was arrested at the age of seventeen for possession with intent to distribute cocaine, and she got off because the charges were dropped. There's an unconfirmed suspicion that her uncle is one of the top Colombian drug lords."

"Where did you get that?"

She flushed. "I can't tell you. Sorry."

"You've hacked into some poor soul's protected files, haven't you?" he asked sternly, but with twinkling eyes.

"I can't tell you," she repeated.

"Okay, I give up." He ate stew and corn bread with obvious enthusiasm. "Then I guess you and I will go on stakeout tomorrow night."

She smiled smugly. "Yes, in your boss's borrowed security car, because my cousin is visiting and we can't neck in the apartment. I told Brody that, and he'll tell Cara that, so if we're seen near my office, they won't think a thing of it."

"Sheer genius," he mused, studying her. "Like I said, you're a natural for law enforcement work. You've got to get your expert computer certification and change professions, Jodie. You're wasted in personnel work."

"Human resources work," she reminded him.

"New label, same job."

She wrinkled her nose. "Maybe so."

They finished their supper in pleasant silence, and she produced a small loaf of pound cake for dessert, with peaches and whipped cream.

"If I ate here often, I'd get fat," he murmured.

She laughed. "Not likely. The cake was made with margarine and reduced-fat milk. I make rolls the same way, except with light olive oil in place of margarine. I don't want clogged arteries before I'm thirty," she added. "And I especially don't want to look like I used to."

He smiled at her warmly. "I like the way you used to look," he said surprisingly. "I like you any way at all, Jodie," he continued softly. "That hasn't changed."

She didn't know whether or not to trust him, and it showed in her face.

He sighed. "It's going to be a long siege," he said enigmatically.

Later, they curled up together on the couch to watch the evening news. There was a brief allusion to a drug smuggling catch by U.S. Customs in the Gulf of Mexico, showing the helicopters they used to catch the fast little boats used in smuggling.

"Those boats go like the wind," Jodie remarked.

He yawned. "They do, indeed. The Colombian National Police busted an operation that was building a submarine for drug smuggling a couple of years ago."

"That's incredible!"

"Some of the smuggling methods are, too, like the tunnel under the Mexican border that was discovered, and having little children swallow balloons filled with cocaine to get them through customs."

"That's barbaric," she said.

He nodded. "It's a profitable business. Greed makes animals of men sometimes, and of women, too."

She cuddled close to him. "It isn't Brody you were after, is it? It's his girlfriend."

He chuckled and wrapped her up in his arms. "You're too sharp for me."

"I learned from an expert," she said, lifting her eyes to his handsome face.

He looked down at her intently for a few seconds before he bent to her mouth and began to kiss her hungrily. Her arms slid up around his neck and she held on for dear life as the kiss devoured her.

Finally he lifted his head and put her away from him, with visible effort. "No more of that tonight," he said huskily.

"Spoilsport," she muttered.

"You're the one with the conscience, honey," he drawled meaningfully. "I'm willing, but you'd never live it down."

"I probably wouldn't," she confessed, but her eyes were misty and wistful.

He pushed back her hair. "Don't look like that," he chided. "It isn't the end of the world. I like you the way you are, Jodie, hang-ups and all. Okay?"

She smiled. "Okay."

"And I'm not sleeping with Kirry!"

The smile grew larger.

He kissed the tip of her nose and got up. "I've got some preparations to make. I'll pick you up tomorrow at 6:20 sharp and we'll park at the warehouse in the under-cover car." He hesitated. "It might be better if I had a female agent in the car with me . . ."

"No, you don't," she said firmly, getting to her feet. "This is my stakeout. You wouldn't even know where to go, or when, if it wasn't for me."

"True. But it could be very dangerous," he added grimly.

"I'm not afraid."

"All right," he said finally. "But you'll stay in the car and out of the line of fire."

"Whatever you say," she agreed at once.

The warehouse parking lot was deserted. The night watchman was visible in the doorway of the warehouse as he opened the door to look out. He did that twice.

"He's in on it," Alexander said coldly, folding Jodie closer in his arms. "He knows they're coming, and he's watching for them."

"No doubt. Ouch." She reached under her rib cage and touched a small hard object in his coat pocket. "What is that, another gun?"

"Another cell phone," he said. "I have two. I'm leaving one with you, in case you see something I don't while I'm inside," he added, indicating a cell phone he'd placed on the dash.

"You do have backup?" she worried.

"Yes. My whole team. They're well concealed, but they're in place."

"Thank goodness!"

He shifted her in his arms so that he could look to his left at the warehouse while he was apparently kissing her.

"Your heart is going very fast," she murmured under his cool lips.

"Adrenaline," he murmured. "I live on rushes of it. I could never settle for a nine to five desk job."

She smiled against his mouth. "I don't like it much, either."

He nuzzled her cheek with his just as a car drove past them toward the warehouse.

It hesitated for a few seconds and then sped on.

"That's Brody's car," she murmured.

"And that one, following it?" he asked, indicating a small red hardtop convertible of some expensive foreign make.

"Cara."

"Amazing that she can afford a Ferrari on thirty-five thousand a year," he mused, "and considering that her mother is poor."

"I was thinking the same thing," she murmured. "Kiss me again."

"No time, honey." He pulled out a two-way radio and spoke into it. "All units, stand by. Target in motion. Repeat, target in motion. Stand by."

Several voices took turns asserting their readiness. Alexander watched as Brody's car suddenly reappeared and he drove away. The gates of the warehouse closed behind his car. He paused near Alexander's car again, and then drove off down the road.

As soon as he was out of sight, a van came into sight. Cara appeared at the parking lot entrance, inserted a card key into the lock, opened the gate and motioned the van forward. The gate didn't close again, but remained open.

Alexander gave it time to get to a loading dock and its occupants to exit the cab and begin opening the rear doors before he took out the walkie-talkie again.

"All units, move in. I repeat, all units, move in. We are good to go!"

He took the cell phone from the dash and put it into Jodie's hands. "You sit right here, with the doors locked, and don't move until I call you on that phone and tell you it's safe. Under no circumstances are you to come into the parking lot. Okay?"

She nodded. "Okay. Don't get shot," she added.

He kissed her. "I don't plan to. See you later."

He got out of the car and went toward a building next door to the warehouse. He was joined by another figure in black. They went down an alley together, out of sight.

Jodie slid down into her seat, so that only her eyes and the top of her head were visible in the concealing darkness, barely lit by a nearby street light. She waited with her heart pounding in her chest for several minutes, until she heard a single gunshot. There was pandemonium in the parking lot. Dark figures ran to and fro. More shots were fired. Her heart jumped into her throat. She gritted her teeth, praying that Alexander wasn't in the line of fire.

Then, suddenly, she spotted him, with

194

another dark figure. They had two people in custody, a man and a woman. They were standing near another loading dock, apparently conversing with the men, when Jodie spotted a solitary figure outside the gates, on the sidewalk, moving toward the open gate. The figure was slight, and it held what looked like an automatic weapon. She'd seen Alexander with one of those, a rare time when he'd been arming himself for a drug bust.

She had a single button to push to make Alexander's cell phone ring, but when she pressed in the number, nothing happened. The phone went dead in her hand.

The man with the machine gun was moving closer to where Alexander and the other man stood with their prisoners, their backs to the gate.

The key was in the car. She only saw one way to save Alexander. She got behind the wheel, cranked the car, put it in gear and aimed it right for the armed man, who was now framed in the gate.

She ran the car at him. He whirled at the sudden noise of an approaching vehicle and started spraying it with machine gun fire.

Jodie ducked down behind the wheel, praying that the weapon didn't have bullets that would penetrate the engine block as easily as they shattered the windshield of the car she was driving. There was a loud thud.

She had to stop the car, because she couldn't see where she was going, but the windshield didn't catch any more bullets. Now she heard gunshots that didn't sound like that of the small automatic her assailant was carrying.

The door of the car was suddenly jerked open, and she looked up, wide-eyed and panicky, into Alexander's white face.

"Jodie!" he ground out. "Put the car out of gear!"

She put it into Park with trembling hands and cut off the ignition.

Alexander dragged her out of it and began going over her with his hands, feeling for blood. She was covered with little shards of glass. Her face was bleeding. So were her hands. She'd put them over her face the instant the man started firing.

Slowly she became aware that Alexander's hands had a faint tremor as they searched her body.

"I'm okay," she said in a thin voice. "Are you?"

"Yes."

But he was rattled, and it showed.

"He was going to shoot you in the back,"

she began.

"I told you to use the cell phone!" he raged.

"It wouldn't work!"

He reached beside her and picked it up. His eyes closed. The battery was dead.

"And you stop yelling at me," she raged back at him. "I couldn't let him kill you!"

He caught her up in his arms, bruisingly close, and kissed her furiously. Then he just held her, rocked her, riveted her to his hard body with fierce hunger. "You crazy woman," he bit off at her ear. "You brave, crazy, wonderful woman!"

She held him, too, content now, safe now. Her eyes closed. It was over, and he was alive. Thank God.

He let her go reluctantly as two other men came up, giving them curious looks.

"She's all right," he told them, moving back a little. "Just a few cuts from the broken windshield."

"That was one of the bravest things I've ever seen a woman do," one of the men, an older man with jet black hair and eyes, murmured. "She drove right into the bullets."

"We'd be dead if she hadn't," the other man, equally dark-haired and dark-eyed, said with a grin. "Thanks!"

"You're welcome," she said with a sheepish smile as she moved closer to Alexander.

"The car's a total write-off," the older man mused.

"Like you've never totaled a car in a gun battle, Hunter," Alexander said with a chuckle.

The other man shrugged. "Maybe one or two. What the hell. The government has all that money we confiscate from drug smugglers to replace cars. You might ask your boss for that cute little Ferrari, Cobb."

"I already drive a Jaguar," he said, laughing. "With all due respect to Ferrari, I wouldn't trade it for anything else."

"I helped make the bust," Jodie complained. "They should give it to me!"

"I wouldn't be too optimistic about that," came a droll remark from the second of the two men. "I think Cobb's boss is partial to Italian sports cars, and he can't afford a Ferrari on his salary."

"Darn," Jodie said on a sigh. "Just my luck."

"You should take her to the hospital and have her checked," Hunter told Alexander. "She's bleeding."

"She could be dead, pulling a stunt like that," Alexander said with renewed anger as he looked at her.

"That's no way to thank a person for saving your life," Jodie pointed out, still riding an adrenaline high.

"You're probably right, but you took a chance you shouldn't have," Alexander said grimly. "Come on. We'll hitch a ride with one of my men."

"Your car might still be drivable," she said, looking at it. The windshield was shattered but still clinging to the frame. She winced. "Or maybe not."

"Maybe not," Alexander agreed. "See you, Hunter. Lane. Thanks for the help."

"Any time," Hunter replied, and they walked back toward the warehouse with Alexander and Jodie. "Colby Lane was in town overnight and bored to death, so I brought him along for the fun."

"Fun!" Jodie exclaimed.

The older man chuckled. "He leads a mundane nine-to-five life. I've talked him into giving it up for international intrigue at Ritter Oil."

"I was just convinced," the man named Colby Lane said with a chuckle.

"Good. Tomorrow you can tell Ritter you'll take the job. See you, Cobb."

"Sure thing."

"Who were those two guys you were talking

to?" Jodie asked when the hospital had treated her cuts and Alexander had commandeered another car to take her home in.

"Phillip Hunter and Colby Lane. You've surely heard of Hunter."

"He's a local legend," she replied with a smile, "but I didn't recognize him in that black garb. He's our security chief."

"Lane's doing the same job for the Hutton corporation, but they're moving overseas and he isn't keen on going. So Hunter's trying to get him to come down here as his second-in-command at Ritter Oil."

"Why was Mr. Lane here tonight?"

"Probably just as Phillip said — Lane just got into town, and Hunter volunteered him to help out. He and Hunter are old friends."

"He looked very dark," she commented.

"They're both Apache," he said easily. "Hunter's married to a knockout blond geologist who works for Ritter. They have a young daughter. Lane's not married."

"They seem to know each other very well."

Alexander chuckled. "They have similar backgrounds in black ops. Highest level covert operations," he clarified. "They used to work for the 'company.' "

"Not Ritter's company," she guessed.

He chuckled. "No. Not Ritter's."

"Did you arrest Cara?"

"Our Houston policewoman made the actual arrest, so that Cara wouldn't know I headed the operation. Cara was arrested along with two men she swears she doesn't know," he replied. "We had probable cause to do a search anyway, but I had a search warrant in my pocket, and I had to use it. We found enough cocaine in there to get a city high, and the two men in the truck had some on them."

"How about Cara?"

He sighed. "She was clean. Now we have to connect her." He glanced at her apologetically. "That will mean getting your boss involved. However innocently, he did let her into a locked parking lot."

"But wasn't the night watchman working for them? Couldn't he have let them in?"

"He could have. But I have a feeling Cara wanted Brody involved, so that he'd be willing to do what she asked so that she didn't give him away for breaking a strict company rule," he replied. He saw her expression and he smiled. "Don't worry. I won't let him be prosecuted."

"Thanks, Alexander."

He moved closer and studied the cuts on her face and arms. He winced. "You poor baby," he said gently. "I wouldn't have had you hurt for the world."

"You'd have been dead if I hadn't done something," she said matter-of-factly. "The phone went dead and you were too far away to hear me if I yelled. Besides," she added with a chuckle, "I hate going to funerals."

"Me, too." He swept her close and kissed the breath out of her. "I have to go back to work, tie up loose ends. You'll need to come with me to the nearest police precinct and give a statement, as well. You're a material witness." He hesitated, frowning.

"What's wrong?" she asked.

"Cara knows who you are, and she can find out where you live," he said. "She's a vengeful witch. Chances are very good that she's going to make bond. I'm going to arrange some security for you."

"Do you think that's necessary?"

He nodded grimly. "I'm afraid it is. Would you like to know the estimated street value of the cocaine we've just confiscated?"

"Yes."

"From thirty to thirty-five million dollars."

She whistled softly. "Now I understand why they're willing to kill people. And that's just one shipment, right?"

"Just one, although it's unusually large. There's another drug smuggling investigation going on right now involving Colombian rebels, but I can't tell you about that one. It's top secret." He smoothed back her hair and looked at her as if she were a treasure trove. "Thank you for what you did," he said after a minute. "Even if it was crazy, it saved my life, not to mention Lane's and Hunter's."

She reached up a soft hand to smooth over his cheek, where it was slightly rough from a day's growth of beard. "You're welcome. But you would have done the same thing, if it had been me, or Margie."

"Yes, I'm afraid I would have."

He still looked worried. She tugged his head down and kissed him warmly, her body exploding inside when he half-lifted her against him and kissed her until her lips were sore.

"I could have lost you tonight," he said curtly.

"Oh, I'm a weed," she murmured into his throat. "We're very hard to uproot."

His arms tightened. "Just the same, you watch your back. If Brody asks what you know, and he will, you tell him nothing," he added. "You were with me when things started happening, you didn't even know what was going on until bullets started flying. Right?"

"Right."

He sighed heavily and kissed her one last

time before he put her back onto her own feet. "I've got to go help the guys with the paperwork," he said reluctantly. "I'd much rather be with you. For tonight, lock your doors and keep your freedom phone handy. If you need me, I'm a phone call away. Tomorrow, you'll have security."

"I've got a nice big heavy flashlight like the one you keep in your car," she told him pertly. "If anybody tries to get in, they'll get a headache."

Unless they had guns, he added silently, but he didn't say that. "Don't be overconfident," he cautioned. "Never underestimate the enemy."

She saluted him.

He tugged her face up and kissed her, hard. "Incorrigible," he pronounced her. "But I can't imagine life without you, so be cautious!"

"I will. I promise. You have to promise, too," she added.

He gave her a warm smile. "Oh, I have my eye on the future, too," he assured her. "I don't plan to cash in my chips right now. I'll phone you tomorrow."

"Okay. Good night."

"Good night. Lock this," he added when he went out the door.

She did, loudly, and heard him chuckle as

he went down the hall. Once he was gone, she sank down into her single easy chair and shivered as she recalled the feverish events of the evening. She was alive. He was alive. But she could still hear the bullets, feel the shattering of the windshield followed by dozens of tiny, painful cuts on her skin even through the sweater she'd been wearing. It was amazing that she'd come out of a firefight with so few wounds.

She went to bed, but she didn't sleep well. Alexander phoned very early the next morning to check on her and tell her that he'd see her at lunch.

She put on her coat and went to work, prepared for some comments from her co-workers, despite the fact that she was wearing a long-sleeved, high-necked blouse. Nothing was going to hide the tiny cuts that lined her cheeks and chin. She knew better than to mention where she got them, so she made up a nasty fall down the steps at her apartment building.

It worked with everyone except Brody. He came in as soon as she'd turned on her computer, looking worried and sad.

"Are you all right?" he asked abruptly. "I was worried sick all night."

Her wide-eyed look wasn't feigned. "How did you know?" she faltered.

"I had to go and bail Cara out of jail early this morning," he said coolly. "She's been accused of drug smuggling, can you imagine it? She was only parking her car when those lunatics opened fire!"

NINE

Remembering what Alexander had cautioned her about, Jodie managed not to laugh out loud at Brody. How could a man be so naive?

"Drug smuggling?" she exclaimed, playing her part. "Cara?"

"That's what they said," he replied. "Apparently some of Ritter's security people had the warehouse staked out. When the shooting started, they returned fire, and I guess they called in the police. In fact, your friend Cobb was there when they arrested Cara."

"Yes, I know. He heard the shooting and walked right into it," she said, choosing her words carefully. "We were parked across the street . . ."

"I saw you when I let Cara into the parking lot," Brody said, embarrassed. "One of the gang came in with a machine gun and they say you aimed Cobb's car right at him and drove into a hail of bullets to save his life. I guess you really do care about him."

"Yes," she confessed. "I do."

"It was a courageous thing to do. Cara said you must be crazy about the guy to do that."

"Poor Cara," she replied, sidestepping the question. "I'm so sorry for the trouble she's in. Why in the world do they think she was involved? She was just in the wrong place at the wrong time."

Brody seemed to relax. "That's what Cara said. Uh, Cobb wasn't in on that bust deliberately, was he?"

"We were in a parked car outside the gate. We didn't know about any bust," she replied.

"So that's why he was there," he murmured absently, nodding. "I thought it must be something of the sort. Cara didn't know any of the others, but one was a female detective and another was a female deputy sheriff. The policewoman arrested her."

"Don't mess with Texas women," Jodie said, adding on a word to the well-known Texas motto.

He laughed. "So it seems. Uh, there was supposed to be a DEA agent there as well. Cara has a friend who works out of the Houston office, but he's been out of town a lot lately and she hasn't been able to contact him. She says it's funny, but he seems to actually be avoiding her." He gave her an odd look. "I gather that it wasn't Cobb. But do you know anything about who the agent was?"

"No," she said straight-faced. "And Alexander didn't mention it, either. He tells me everything, so I'd know if it was him."

"I see."

She wondered if Cara's friend at the DEA was named Kennedy, but she pretended to know nothing. "What's Cara going to do?" she asked, sounding concerned.

"Get a good lawyer, I suppose," he said heavily.

"I wish her well. I'm so sorry, Brody."

He sighed heavily. "I seem to have a knack for getting myself into tight corners, but I think Cara's easily superior to me in that respect. Well, I'd better phone the attorney whose name she gave me. You're sure you're all right?"

"I'm fine, Brody, honestly." She smiled at him.

He smiled back. "See you."

She watched him go with relief. She'd been improvising widely to make sure he didn't connect Alexander with the surveillance of the warehouse.

■ ■ ■ ■

When Alexander phoned her, she arranged to meet him briefly at the café downstairs for coffee. He was pushed for time, having been in meetings with his drug unit most of the day planning strategy.

"You've become a local legend," he told her with a mischievous smile when they were drinking cappuccino.

"Me?" she exclaimed.

He grinned at her. "The oil clerk who drove through a hail of bullets to save her lover."

She flushed and glared at him. "Point one, I am not a clerk, I'm an administrative assistant. And point two, I am not your — !"

"I didn't say I started the rumor." He chuckled. His eyes became solemn as he studied her across the table. "But the part about being a heroine, I endorse enthusiastically. That being said, would you like to add to your legend?"

She paid attention. "Are you kidding? What do you want me to do?"

"Cara made bond this afternoon," he told her. "We've got a tail on her, but she's sure to suspect that. She'll make contact with one of her subordinates, in some public place where she thinks we won't be able to tape her. When she does, I'm going to want you to accidentally happen upon her and plant a microphone under her table."

"Wow! 'Jane Bond' stuff!"

"Jane?" he wondered.

She shrugged. "A woman named James would be a novelty."

"Point taken. Are you game?"

"Of course. But why wouldn't you let one of your own people do it?"

His face was revealing. "The last hearty professional we sent to do that little task stumbled over his own feet and pitched headfirst into the table our target was occupying. In the process he overturned a carafe of scalding coffee, also on the target, who had to be taken to the hospital for treatment."

"What if I do the same thing?" she worried.

He smiled gently. "You don't have a clumsy bone in your body, Jodie. But even if you did, Cara knows you. She might suspect me, but she won't suspect you."

"When do I start?"

"I'll let you know," he promised. "In the meantime, keep your eyes and ears open, and don't . . ."

Just as he spoke, there was a commotion

outside the coffee shop. A young woman with long blond hair was trailing away a dark-haired little girl with a shocked face. Behind them, one of the men Jodie recognized from the drug bust — one of Alexander's friends — was waving his arms and talking loudly in a language Jodie had never heard before, his expression furious.

The trio passed out of sight, but not before Jodie finally recognized the man Alexander had called Colby Lane.

"What in the world . . . ?" she wondered.

"It's a long story," Alexander told her. "And I'm not at liberty to repeat it. Let's just say that Colby has been rather suddenly introduced to a previously unknown member of his family."

"Was he cursing — and in what language?" she persisted.

"You can't curse in Apache," he assured her. "It's like Japanese — if you really want to tick somebody off in Japan, you say something about their mother's belly button. But giving them the finger doesn't have any meaning."

"Really?" She was fascinated.

He chuckled. "Anyway, Native Americans — whose origins are also suspected to be Asian — don't use curse words in their own language."

"Mr. Lane looked very upset. And I thought I recognized that blond woman. She was transferred here from their Arizona office just a few weeks ago. She has a little girl, about the same age as Mr. Hunter's daughter."

"Let it lie," Alexander advised. "We have problems of our own. I meant to mention that we've located one of Cara's known associates serving as a waiter in a little coffeehouse off Alameda called 'The Beat' . . ."

"I go there!" she exclaimed. "I go there a lot! You can get all sorts of fancy coffees and it's like a retro 'beatnik' joint. They play bongos and wear all black and customers get up and read their poetry." She flushed. "I actually did that myself, just last week."

He was impressed. "You, getting up in front of people to read poetry? I didn't know you still wrote poetry, Jodie."

"It's very personal stuff," she said, uneasy.

He began to look arrogant. "About me?"

She glared at him. "At the time I wrote it, you were my least favorite person on the planet," she informed him.

"Ouch!" He was thinking again. "But if they already know you there, it's even less of a stretch if you show up when Cara does — assuming she even uses the café for her purposes. We'll have to wait and see. I don't expect her to arrange a rendezvous with a colleague just to suit me."

"Nice of you," she teased.

He chuckled. He reached across the table and linked her fingers with his. His green eyes probed hers for a long moment. "Those cuts are noticeable on your face," he said quietly. "Do they hurt?"

"Not nearly as much as having you gunned down in front of me would have," she replied.

His eyes began to glitter with feeling. His fingers contracted around hers. "Which is just how I felt when I saw those bullets slamming into the windshield of my car, with you at the wheel."

Her breath caught. He'd never admitted so much in the past.

He laughed self-consciously and released her hand. "We're getting morose. A miss is as good as a mile, and I still have paperwork to finish that I haven't even started on." He glanced at his watch. "I can't promise anything, but we might see a movie this weekend."

"That would be nice," she said. "You'll let me know . . . ?"

He frowned. "I don't like putting you in the line of fire a second time."

"I go to the coffee shop all the time," she

reminded him. "I'm not risking anything." Except my heart, again, she thought.

He sighed. "I suppose so. Just the same, don't let down your guard. I hope you can tell if someone's tailing you?"

"I get goose bumps on the back of my neck," she assured him. "I'll be careful. You do the same," she added firmly.

He smiled gently. "I'll do my best."

Having settled down with a good book the following day after a sandwich and soup supper, it was a surprise to have Alexander phone her and ask her to go down to the coffee shop on the double.

"I'll meet you in the parking lot with the equipment," he said. "Get a cab and have it drop you off. I'll reimburse you. Hurry, Jodie."

"Okay. I'm on my way," she promised, lounging in pajamas and a robe.

She dashed into the bedroom, threw on a long black velvet skirt, a black sweater, loafers, and ran a quick brush through her loosed hair before perching her little black beret on top of her head. She grabbed her coat and rushed out the door, barely pausing except to lock it. She was at the elevator before she remembered her purse, lying on the couch. She dashed back to get it, cursing her own lack of preparedness in an emergency.

Minutes later, she got out of the cab at the side door of The Beat coffeehouse.

Alexander waited by his company car while Jodie paid the cab. She joined him, careful to notice that she was unobserved.

He straightened at her approach. In the well-lit parking lot, she could see his eyes. They were troubled.

"I'm here," she said, just for something to say. "What do you want me to do?"

"I'm not sure I want you to do anything," he said honestly. "This is dangerous. Right now, she has no reason to suspect you. But if you bug her table for me, and she finds out that you did, your life could be in danger."

"Hey, listen, you were the one who told me about the little boys being shot by her henchmen," she reminded him. "I know the risk, Alexander. I'm willing to take it."

"Your knees are knocking," he murmured.

She laughed, a little unsteadily. "I guess they are. And my heart's pounding. But I'm still willing to do it. Now what exactly do I do?"

He opened the passenger door for her. "Get in. I'll brief you."

"Is she here?" she asked when they were inside.

"Yes. She's at the table nearest the kitchen door, at the left side of the stage. Here." He handed her a fountain pen.

"No, thanks," she said, waving it away. "I've got two in my purse . . ."

He opened her hand and placed the capped pen in it. She looked at it, surprised by its heaviness. "It's a miniature receiver," he told her. He produced a small black box with an antenna, and what looked like an earplug with a tiny wire sticking out the fat end. "The box is a receiver, linked to a tape recorder. The earplug is also a receiver, which we use when we're in close quarters and don't want to attract attention. Since the box has a range of several hundred feet, I'll be able to hear what comes into the pen from my car."

"Do you want me to accidentally leave the pen on her table?"

"I want you to accidentally drop it under her table," he said. "If she sees it, the game's up. We're not the only people who deal in counterespionage."

She sucked in her breath. She was getting the picture. Cara was no dummy. "Okay. I'll lean over her table to say hello and make sure I put it where she won't feel it with her foot. How will that do?"

"Yes. But you have to make sure she doesn't see you do it."

"I'll be very careful."

He was having second thoughts. She was brave, but courage wasn't the only requirement for such an assignment. He remembered her driving through gunfire to save him. She could have died then. He'd thought about little else, and he hadn't slept well. Jodie was like a silver thread that ran through his life. In recent weeks, he'd been considering, seriously, how hard it would be to go on without her. He wasn't certain that he could.

"Why are you watching me like that?" she wanted to know, smiling curiously. "I'm not a dummy. I won't let you down, honest."

"It wasn't that." He closed her fingers around the pen. "Are you sure you want to go through with this?"

"Very sure."

"Okay." He hesitated. "What are you going to give as an excuse for being there?"

She gave him a bright smile. "I phoned Johnny — the owner — earlier, just after you phoned me and told him I had a new poem, but I was a little nervous about getting up in front of a big crowd. He said there was only a small crowd and I'd do fine."

"You improvise very well."

"I've been observing you for years," she teased. "But it's true. I do have a poem to read, which should throw Cara off the track."

He tugged her chin up and kissed her, hard. "You're going to be fine."

She smiled at him. "Which one of us are you supposed to be reassuring?"

"Both of us," he said tenderly. He kissed her again. "Go to work."

"What do I do when she leaves?"

"Get a cab back to your apartment. I'll meet you there. If anything goes wrong," he added firmly, "or if she acts suspicious, you stay in the coffeehouse and phone my cell number. Got that?" He handed her a card with his mobile phone number on it.

"I've got it."

She opened the car door and stepped out into the cool night air. With a subdued wave, she turned, pulled her coat closer around her and walked purposefully toward the coffeehouse. What she didn't tell Alexander was that her new poem was about him.

She didn't look around noticeably as she made her way through the sparse crowd to the table where she usually sat on her evenings here. She held the pen carefully in her hand, behind a long fold of her coat. As she pulled out a chair at the table, her eyes swept the room and she spotted Cara at a table with another woman. She smiled and Cara frowned.

Uh-oh, she thought, but she pinned the smile firmly to her face and moved to Cara's table.

"I thought it was you," she said cheerily. "I didn't know you ever came here! Brody never mentioned it to me."

Cara gave her a very suspicious look. "This is not your normal evening entertainment, surely?"

"But I come here all the time," Jodie replied honestly. "Johnny's one of my fans."

"Fans." Cara turned the word over on her tongue as if she'd never heard it.

"Aficionados," Jodie persisted. "I write poetry."

"You?"

The other woman made it sound like an insult. The woman beside her, an even older woman with a face like plate steel, only looked.

Jodie felt a chill of fear and worked to hide it. Her palm sweated against the weight of the pen hidden in her hand. As she hesitated, Johnny came walking over in his apron.

"Hey, Jodie!" he greeted. "Now don't worry, there's only these two unfamiliar ladies in here, you know everybody else. You just get up there and give it your best. It'll be great!"

"Johnny, you make me feel so much better," she told the man.

"These ladies friends of yours?" he asked, noticing them — especially Cara — with interested dark eyes.

"Cara's boyfriend is my boss at work," Jodie said.

"Lucky boyfriend," Johnny murmured, his voice dropping an octave.

Cara relaxed and smiled. "I am Cara Dominguez," she introduced herself. "This is my *amiga*, Chiva."

Johnny leaned over the table to shake hands and Jodie pretended to be overbalanced by him. In the process of righting herself and accepting his apology, she managed to let the pen drop under the table where it lay unnoticed several inches from either woman's foot.

"Sorry, Jodie, meeting two such lovely ladies made me clumsy." He chuckled.

She grinned at him. "No harm done. I'm not hurt."

"Okay, then, you go get on that stage. Want your usual French Vanilla cappuccino?"

"You bet. Make it a large one, with a croissant, please."

"It'll be on the house," he informed her. "That's incentive for you."

"Gee, thanks!" she exclaimed.

"My treat. Nice to meet you ladies."

"It is for us the same," Cara purred. She glanced at Jodie, much less suspicious now. "So you write poetry. I will enjoy listening to it."

Jodie chuckled. "I'm not great, but people here are generally kind. Good to see you."

Cara shrugged. The other woman said nothing.

Jodie pulled off her coat and went up onto the stage, trying to ignore her shaking knees. Meanwhile she prayed that Alexander could hear what the two women were saying. Because the minute she pulled the microphone closer, introduced herself, and pulled out the folded sheet of paper that contained her poem, Cara leaned toward the other woman and started speaking urgently.

Probably exchanging fashion tips, or some such thing, Jodie thought dismally, but she smiled at the crowd, unfolded the paper, and began to read.

Apparently her efforts weren't too bad, because the small crowd paid attention to every line of the poem. And when she finished reading it, there was enthusiastic applause.

Cara and her friend, however, were much too intent on conversation to pay Jodie any attention. She went back to her seat, ate her croissant and drank her cappuccino with her back to the table where Cara and the other woman were sitting, just to make sure they knew she wasn't watching them.

A few minutes later, Johnny came by her table and patted her on the back. "That was some good work, girl!" he exclaimed. "I'm sorry your friend didn't seem to care enough to listen to it."

"She's not into poetry," she confided.

"I guess not. She and that odd-looking friend of hers didn't even finish their coffee."

"They're gone?" she asked without turning.

He nodded. "About five minutes ago, I guess. No great loss, if you ask me."

"Thanks for the treat, Johnny, and for the encouragement," she added.

"Um, I sure would like to have a copy of that poem."

Her eyes widened. "You would? Honestly?"

He shrugged. "It was really good. I know this guy. He works for a small press. They publish poetry. I'd like to show it to him. If you don't mind."

"Mind!" She handed him the folded paper. "I don't mind! Thanks, Johnny!"

"No problem. I'll be in touch." He turned, and then paused, digging into his apron pocket. "Say, is this yours? I'm afraid I may have stepped on it. It was under that table where your friend was sitting."

"Yes, it's mine," she said, taking it from him. "Thanks a lot."

He winced. "If I broke it, I'll buy you a new one, okay?"

"It's just a pen," she said with determined carelessness. "No problem."

"You wait, I'll call you a cab."

"That would be great!"

She settled back to wait, her head full of hopeful success, and not only for Alexander.

"Is it broken?" she asked Alexander when she was back at her apartment, and he was examining his listening device.

"I'll have the lab guys check it out," he told her.

"Could you hear anything?"

He grinned hugely. "Not only did I hear plenty, I taped it. We've got a lead we'd never have had without you. There's just one bad thing."

"Oh?"

"Cara thinks your poetry stinks," he said with a twinkle in his eyes.

"She can think what she likes, but Johnny's showing it to a publisher friend of his. He thought it was wonderful."

He searched her face. "So did I, Jodie."

She felt a little nervous, but certainly he couldn't have known that he was the subject of it, so she just thanked him offhandedly.

"Now I'm sure I'm cut out for espionage," she murmured.

"You may be, but I don't know if my nerves could take it."

"You thought I'd mess up," she guessed.

He shook his head, holding her hand firmly in his. "It wasn't that. I don't like having you at risk, Jodie. I don't want you on the firing line ever again, even if you did save my skin last night."

She searched his green eyes hungrily. "I wouldn't want to live in a world that didn't contain you, too," she said. Then, backtracking out of embarrassment, she laughed and added, "I really couldn't live without the aggravation."

He laughed, as he was meant to. "Same here." He checked his watch. "I don't want to go," he said unexpectedly, "but I've got to get back to my office and go through this tape. Tomorrow, I'll be in conference with my drug unit. You pretend that nothing at all was amiss, except you saw Cara at your favorite evening haunt. Right?"

"Right," she assured him.

"I'll call you."

"That's what they all say," she said dryly.

He paused at the door and looked at her. "Who?"

"Excuse me?"

"Who else is promising to call you?" he persisted.

"The president, for my advice on his foreign policy, of course," she informed him.

He laughed warmly. "Incorrigible," he said to himself, winked at her, and let himself out. "Lock it!" he called through it.

She snicked the lock audibly and heard him chuckle again. She leaned back against the door with a relieved sigh. It was over. She'd done what he asked her, and she hadn't fouled it up. Most of all, he was pleased with her.

She was amazed at the smiles she got from him in recent weeks. He'd always been reserved, taciturn, with most other people.

But he enjoyed her company and it showed.

The next day, Brody seemed very pre-occupied. She took dictation, which he gave haltingly, and almost absently.

"Are you okay?" she wanted to know.

He moved restively around his office. He turned to stare at her curiously. "Are you involved in some sort of top secret operation or something?"

Her eyes popped. "Pardon?"

He cleared his throat. "I know you were at a coffeehouse where Cara went last night with a friend. I wondered if you were spying on her . . . ?"

"I go to The Beat all the time, Brody," she told him, surprised. "Alexander's idea of an evening out is a concert or the theater, but my tastes run to bad poetry and bongos. I've been going there for weeks. It's no secret. The owner knows me very well."

He relaxed suddenly and smiled. "Thank goodness! That's what Cara told me, of course, but it seemed odd that you'd be there when she was. I mean, like you and your boyfriend showed up at the restaurant where we had lunch that day, and then you were at the concert, too. And your friend does work for the DEA . . ."

"Coincidences," she said lazily. "That's

all. Unless you think I've been following you," she added with deliberate emphasis, demurely lowering her eyes.

There was a long, shocked pause. "Why, I never thought . . . considered . . . really?"

She crossed her legs. "I think you're very nice, Brody, and Cara treats you like a pet dog," she said with appropriate indignation. She peered at him covertly. "You're too good for her."

He was obviously embarrassed, flattered, and uncertain. "My gosh . . . I'm sorry, but I knew about Cobb working for the DEA, and then the drug bust came so unexpectedly. Well, it seemed logical that he might be spying on Cara with your help . . ."

"I never dreamed that I looked like a secret agent!" she exclaimed, and then she chuckled. "As if Alexander would ever trust me with something so dangerous," she added, lowering her eyes so that he couldn't see them.

He sighed. "Forgive me. I've had these crazy theories. Cara thought I was nuts, especially after she told me the owner of that coffeehouse knew you very well and encouraged you to read . . . well . . . very bad poetry. She thought maybe he had a case on you."

"It was not bad poetry! And he had a case

on Cara, not me," she replied with just the right amount of pique.

"Did he!"

"I told him she was your girlfriend, don't worry," she said, and managed to sound regretful.

"Jodie, I'm very flattered," he faltered.

She held up a hand. "Let's not talk about it, Brody, okay? You just dictate, and I'll write."

He sighed, studying her closely. After a minute, he shrugged, and began dictating. This time, he was concise and relaxed. Jodie felt like collapsing with relief, herself. It had been a close call, and not even because Cara was suspicious. It was Brody who seemed to sense problems.

TEN

It was a relief that Cara didn't suspect Jodie of spying, but it was worrying that Brody did. He was an intelligent man, and it wouldn't be easy to fool him. She'd have to mention that to Alexander when she saw him.

He came by the apartment that evening, soon after Jodie got home from work, taciturn and worried.

"Something happened," she guessed uneasily.

He nodded. "Got any coffee?"

"Sure. Come on into the kitchen."

He sat down and she poured him a cup from the pot full she'd just made. He sipped it and studied her across the table. "Kennedy came back to town today. He's Cara's contact."

"Oh, dear," she murmured, sensing that something was very wrong.

He nodded. "I called him into my office

and told him I was firing him, and why. I have sworn statements from two witnesses who are willing to testify against him in return for reduced sentences." He sighed. "He said that he knew you were involved, that you'd helped me finger Cara, and that he'd tell her if I didn't back down."

"Don't feel bad about it," she said, mentally panicking while trying not to show it. "You couldn't let him stay, after what he did."

He looked at her blankly. "You're a constant surprise to me, Jodie. How did you know I wouldn't back down?"

She smiled gently. "You wouldn't be Alexander if you let people bluff you."

"Yes, baby, but he's not bluffing."

The endearment caught her off guard, made her feel warm inside, warm all over. "So what do we do now?" she asked, a little disconcerted.

He noted her warm color and smiled tenderly. "You go live with Margie for a few days, until I wrap up this case. Our cover's blown now for sure."

"Margie can shoot a gun, but she's not all that great at it, Alexander," she pointed out.

"Our foreman, Chayce, is, and so is cousin Derek," he replied. "He was involved in national security work when he was just out of college. He's a dead shot, and he'll be bringing his two brothers with him." He chuckled. "Funny. All I had to say was that Margie might be in danger along with you, and he volunteered at once."

"You don't like him," she recalled.

He shrugged. "I don't like the idea of Margie getting involved with a cousin. But Derek seemed to know that, too, and he told me something I didn't know before when I phoned him. He wasn't my uncle's son. His mother had an affair with an old beau and he was the result. It was a family secret until last night. Which means," he added, "that he's only related to us by marriage, not by blood."

"He told you himself?" she asked.

"He told me. Apparently, he told you, too. But he didn't tell Margie."

"Have you?" she wondered.

"That's for him to do," he replied. "I've interfered enough." He checked his watch. "I've got to go. I have a man watching the apartment," he added. "The one I told you about. But tomorrow, you tell Brody you're taking a few days off to look after a sick relative and you go to Margie. Got that?"

"But my job . . . !"

"It's your life!" he shot back, eyes blazing. "This is no game. These people will kill you as surely as they killed those children. I am not going to watch you die, Jodie. Least of all for something I got you into!"

She caught her breath. This was far more serious than she'd realized.

"I told you," he emphasized, "Cara knows you were involved. The secret's out. You leave town. Period."

She stared at him and knew she was trapped. Her job was going to be an after-thought. They'd fire her. She was even afraid to take a day off when she was sick, because the company policy in her depart-ment was so strict.

"If you lose that job, it will be a blessing," Alexander told her flatly. "You're too good to waste your life taking somebody else's dictation. When this is over, I'll help you find something better. I'll take you to classes so that you can get your expert computer certification, then I'll get an employment agency busy to find you a better job."

That was a little disappointing. Obviously he didn't have a future with her in mind, or he wouldn't be interested in getting her a job.

He leaned back in his chair, sipping cof-fee. "Although," he added suddenly, his gaze intent, "there might be an alternative."

"An alternative?"

"We'll talk about that later," he said. He finished his coffee. "I have to go."

She got up and walked him to the door. "You be careful, too," she chided.

He opened his jacket and indicated the .45 automatic in its hand-tooled leather holster.

"It won't shoot itself," she reminded him pertly.

He chuckled, drew her into his arms, and kissed her until her young body ached with deep, secret longings.

He lifted his head finally, and he wasn't breathing normally. She felt the intensity of his gaze all the way to her toes as he looked at her. "All these years," he murmured, "and I wasted them sniping at you."

"You seemed to enjoy it at the time," she remarked absently, watching his mouth hover over hers.

"I didn't want a marriage like my parents had. I played the field, to keep women from getting serious about me," he confessed. He traced her upper lip with his mouth, with breathless tenderness. "Especially you," he added roughly. "No one else posed the threat you did, with your old-fashioned ideals and your sterling character. But I couldn't let you see how attracted to you I was. I did a pretty good job. And then you had too much champagne at a party and did what I'd been afraid you'd do since you graduated from high school."

"You were afraid . . . ?"

He nibbled her upper lip. "I knew that if you ever got close, I'd never be able to let you go," he whispered sensuously. "What I spouted to Margie was a lot of hot air. I ached from head to toe after what we did together. I wanted you so badly, honey. I didn't sleep all night thinking about how easy it would have been."

"I didn't sleep thinking that you hated me," she confessed.

He sighed regretfully. "I didn't know you'd overheard me, but I said enough when I left you at your bedroom. I felt guilty when I went downstairs and saw your face. You were shamed and humiliated, and it was my fault. I only wanted a chance to make amends, but you started backing away and you wouldn't stop. That was when I knew what a mistake I'd made."

She toyed with his shirt button. "And then you needed help to catch a drug smuggler," she mused.

There was a pause long enough to make her look up. "You're good, Jodie, and I did need somebody out of the agency to dig out that information for me. But . . ."

"But?"

He smiled sheepishly. "Houston P.D. owes me a favor. They'd have been glad to get the information for me. So would the Texas Rangers, or the county sheriff."

"Then why did you ask me to do it?" she exclaimed.

His hands went to frame her face. They felt warm and strong against her soft skin. "I was losing you," he whispered as he bent again to rub his lips tenderly over her mouth. "You wouldn't let me near you any other way."

His mouth was making pudding of her brain. She slid her arms up around his neck and her hands tangled in the thick hair above his nape. "But there was Kirry . . ."

"Window dressing. I didn't even like her, especially by the time my birthday rolled around. I gave Margie hell for inviting her to my birthday party, did she tell you?"

She shook her head, dazed.

He caught her upper lip in his mouth and toyed with it. His breathing grew unsteady. His hands on her face became insistent. "I got drunk when Margie told me you'd overheard us," he whispered. "It took two neat whiskeys for me to even phone you. Too much was riding on my ability to make an apology. And frankly, baby, I don't make a habit of giving them."

She melted into his body, hungry for closer contact. "I was so ashamed of what I'd done . . ."

His mouth crushed down onto hers with passionate intent. "I loved what you did," he ground out. "I wasn't kidding when I told you that. I could taste you long after I went to bed. I dreamed about it all night."

"So did I," she whispered.

His lips parted hers ardently. "I thought you were hung up on damned Brody," he murmured, "until you aimed that car at the gunman. I prayed for all I was worth until I got to you and knew that you were all right. I could have lost you forever. It haunts me!"

"I'm tougher than old cowboy boots," she whispered, elated beyond belief at what he was saying to her.

"And softer than silk, in all the right places. Come here." He moved her against the wall. His body pressed hers gently against it while he kissed her with all the pent-up longing he'd been suppressing for weeks. When she moaned, he felt his body tremble with aching need.

"You're killing me," he ground out.

"Wh . . . what?"

He lifted his head and looked down into soft, curious brown eyes. "You haven't got a clue," he muttered. "Can't you tell when a man's dying of lust?"

Her eyebrows arched as he rested his weight on his hands next to her ears on the wall and suddenly pressed his hips into hers, emphatically demonstrating the question.

She swallowed hard. "Alexander, I was really only kidding about having a dress with prophylactics pinned to the hem. . . ."

He burst out laughing and forced his aching body away from hers. "I've never laughed as much in my life as I do with you," he said on a long sigh. "But I really would give half an arm to lay you down on the carpet right now, Jodie."

She flushed with more delight than fear. "One of us could run to the drugstore, I guess," she murmured dryly.

"Not now," he whispered wickedly. "But hold that thought until I wind up this case."

She laughed. "Okay."

He nibbled her upper lip. "I'll pick you up at work about nine in the morning," he murmured as he lifted his head. "And I'll drive you down to Jacobsville."

"You're really worried," she realized, when she saw the somber expression.

"Yes, Jodie. I'm really worried. Keep your doors locked and don't answer the phone."

"What if it's you?" she worried.

"Do you still have the cell phone I loaned you?"

"Yes."

She produced it. He opened it, turned it on, and checked the battery. "It's fully charged. Leave it on. If I need to call you, I'll use this number. You can call me if you're afraid. Okay?"

"Okay."

He kissed her one last time, gave her a soulful, enigmatic look, and went out the door. She bolted it behind him and stood there for several long seconds, her head whirling with the changes that were suddenly upsetting her life and career. Alexander was trying to tell her something, but she couldn't quite decide what. Did he want an affair? He certainly couldn't be thinking about marriage, he hated the whole thought of it. But, what did he want? She worried the question until morning, and still had no answers.

"You're going to leave for three days, just like that?" Brody exploded at work the next morning, his face harder than Jodie had ever seen it. "How the hell am I going to manage without a secretary?" he blustered. "I can't type my own letters!"

The real man, under the facade, Jodie

thought, fascinated with her first glimpse of Brody's dark side. She'd never seen him really angry.

"I'm not just a secretary," she reminded him.

"Oh, hell, you do mail and requisition forms," he said coldly. "Call it what you like, it's donkey work." His eyes narrowed. "It's because of what you did to Cara, isn't it? You're scared, so you're running away!"

Her face flamed with temper. She stood up from her desk and gave him a look that would have melted steel. "Would you be keen to hang around if they were gunning for you? You listen to me, Brody, these drug lords don't care who dies as long as they get their money. There are two dead little children who didn't do a thing wrong, except stand between a drug dealer and their mother, who was trying to shut down drug dealing in her neighborhood. Cara is part of that sick trade, and if you defend her, so are you!"

He gaped at her. In the years they'd worked together, Jodie had never talked back to him.

She grabbed up her purse and got the few personal belongings out of her desk. "Never mind holding my job open for me. I quit!" she told him flatly. "There must be more to life than pandering to the ego of a man who thinks I'm a donkey. One more thing, Brody," she added, facing him with her arms full of her belongings. "You and your drug-dealing girlfriend can both go to hell, with my blessing!"

She turned and stalked out of her cubicle. She imagined a trail of fire behind her. Brody's incredulous gasp had been music to her ears. Alexander was right. She was wasted here. She'd find something better, she knew it.

On her way out the door, she almost collided with Phillip Hunter. He righted her, his black eyebrows arching.

"You're leaving, Miss Clayburn?" he asked.

"I'm leaving, Mr. Hunter," she said, still bristling from her encounter with Brody.

"Great. Come with me."

He motioned with his chin. She followed him, puzzled, because he'd never spoken to her before except in a cordial, impersonal way.

He led her into the boardroom and closed the door. Inside was the other dark man she'd met briefly during the drug bust at the warehouse, Colby Lane, and the owner of the corporation himself, Eugene Ritter.

"Sit down, Ms. Clayburn," Ritter said with

a warm smile, his blue eyes twinkling under a lock of silver hair.

She dropped into a chair, with her sack full of possessions clutched close to her chest.

"Mr. Ritter," she began, wondering what in the world she was going to do now. "I can explain . . ."

"You don't have to," he said gently. "I already know everything. When this drug case is wrapped up — and Cobb assures me it will be soon — how would you like to come back and work for me in an area where your skills won't be wasted?"

She was speechless. She just stared at him over her bulging carry-all.

"Phillip wants to go home to Arizona to work in our branch office there, and Colby Lane here —" he indicated the other dark man "— is going to replace him. He knows about your computer skills and Cobb's already told him that you're a whiz with investigations. How would you like to work for Lane as a computer security consultant? It will pay well and you'll have autonomy within the corporation. The downside," he added slowly, "is that you may have to do some traveling eventually, to our various branch offices, to work with Hunter and our other troubleshooters. Is that a problem?"

She shook her head, still grasping for a hold on the situation.

"Good!" He rubbed his hands together. "Then we'll draw up a contract for you, and you can have your attorney read and approve it when you come back." He was suddenly solemn. "There are going to be a lot of changes here in the near future. I've been coasting along in our headquarters office in Oklahoma and letting the outlying divisions take care of themselves, with near-disastrous results. If Hunter hadn't been tipped off by Cobb about the warehouse being used as a drug drop, we could have been facing federal charges, with no intentional involvement whatsoever on our part, on international drug smuggling. Tell Cobb we owe him one for that."

She grinned. "I will. And, Mr. Ritter, thank you very much for the opportunity. I won't let you down."

"I know that, Ms. Clayburn," he told her, smiling back. "Hunter will walk you outside. Just in case. Not that I think you need too much protection," he added, tongue-in-cheek. "There aren't a lot of people who'll drive into gunfire to save another person."

She laughed. "If I'd had time to think about it, I probably wouldn't have done it. Just the same, I won't mind having an escort to the front entrance," she confessed, standing. "I'm getting a cab to my apartment."

"We'll talk again," Ritter assured her, standing. He was tall and very elegant in a gray business suit. "All right, come on, Lane. We'll inspect the warehouse one last time."

"Yes, sir," Lane agreed.

"I'm just stunned," Jodie murmured when they reached the street, where the cab she'd called was waiting. She'd also phoned Cobb to meet her at her apartment.

"Ritter sees more than people think he does," Hunter told her, chuckling. "He's sharp, and he doesn't miss much. Tell Cobb I owe him one, too. My wife and I have been a little preoccupied lately — we just found out that we're expecting again. My mind hasn't been as much on the job as it should have been."

"Congratulations!"

He shrugged. "I wouldn't mind another girl, but Jennifer wants a son this time, a matched set, she calls it. She wants to be near her cousin Danetta, who's also expecting a second child. She and Cabe Ritter, the old man's son, have a son but they want a daughter." He chuckled. "We'll see what we both get. Meanwhile, you go straight to your apartment with no stops," he directed, becoming solemn. He looked over the top of the cab, saw something, and nodded approvingly. "Cobb's having you tailed. No, don't look back. If anyone makes a try for you, dive for cover and let your escort handle it, okay?"

"Okay. But I'm not really nervous about it now."

"So I saw the other night," he replied. "You've got guts, Ms. Clayburn. You'll be a welcome addition to security here."

She beamed. "I'll do my best. Thanks again."

"No problem. Be safe."

He closed the door and watched the taxi pull away. Her escort, in a dark unmarked car, pulled right out behind the cab. She found herself wishing that Cara and her group would make a try for her. It wouldn't bother her one bit to have the woman land in jail for a long time.

Alexander was waiting for her at her apartment. He picked up the suitcase she'd packed and then he drove her down to the Jacobsville ranch. She didn't have time to tell him about the changes in her life. She was saving that for a surprise. She was feeling good about her own abilities, and her confidence in herself had a surprising effect on her friend Margie, who met her at the door with faint shock.

Margie hugged her, but her eyes were wary. "There's something different about you," she murmured sedately.

"I've been exercising," she assured the other woman amusedly.

"Sure she has." Alexander chuckled. "By aiming cars at men armed with automatic weapons."

"What!" Margie exclaimed, gasping.

"Well, they were shooting at Alexander," Jodie told her. "What else could I do?"

Margie and her brother exchanged a long, serious look. He nodded slowly, and then he smiled. Margie beamed.

"What's that all about?" Jodie wondered aloud.

"We're passing along mental messages," Margie told her with wicked eyes. "Never mind. You're just in time to try on the flamenco dress I made you for our Halloween party."

"Halloween party." Jodie nodded blankly.

"It's this Saturday," Margie said, exasperated. "We always have it the weekend before Halloween, remember?"

"I didn't realize it was that far along in the month," Jodie said. "I guess I've been busier than I realized."

"She writes poetry about me," Alexander said as he went up the staircase with Jodie's bag.

"I do not write poetry about you!" Jodie called after him.

He only laughed. "And she reads it on stage in a retro beatnik coffeehouse."

"For real?" Margie asked. "Jodie, I have to come stay with you in Houston so you can take me there. I love coffeehouses and poetry!" She shook her head. "I can't imagine you reading poetry on a stage. Or driving a car into bullets, for that matter." She looked shocked. "Jodie, you've changed."

Jodie nodded. "I guess I have."

Margie hugged her impulsively. "Are we still friends?" she wondered. "I haven't been a good one, but I'm going to try. I can actually make canapés!" she added. "I took lessons. So now you can come to parties when Jessie's not here, and I won't even ask you to do any of the work!"

Jodie burst out laughing. "This I have to see."

"You can, Friday. I expect it will take all day, what with the decorating, and I'm doing all that myself, too. Derek thinks I'm improving madly," she added, and a faint flush came to her cheeks.

"Cousin Derek's here already?" she asked.

"He's not actually my cousin at all, except by marriage, although I only just found out," Margie said, drawing Jodie along with her into the living room. "He's got two brothers and they're on the way here. One of them is a cattle rancher and the other is a divorced grizzly bear."

"A what?"

Margie looked worried. "He's a Bureau of Land Management enforcement agent," she said. "He tracks down poachers and people who deal in illegal hunting and such. He's the one whose wife left him for a car salesman. He's very bitter."

"Is Derek close to them?"

"To the rancher one," Margie said. "He doesn't see the grizzly bear too often, thank goodness."

"Thank goodness?" Jodie probed delicately.

Margie flushed. "I think Cousin Derek wants to be much more than my cousin."

"It's about time," Jodie said with a wicked smile. "He's just your type."

Margie made a face. "Come on into the kitchen and we'll see what there is to eat. I don't know about you, but I'm hungry." She stopped suddenly. "Don't take this the wrong way, but why are Derek and his brothers moving in and why are you and Alexander here in the middle of the week?"

"Oh, somebody's just going to try to kill me, that's all," Jodie said matter-of-factly. "But Alexander's more than able to handle them, with Cousin Derek's help and some hard work by the DEA and Alexander's drug unit."

"Trying to kill you." Margie nodded. "Right."

"That's no joke," Alexander said from the doorway. He came into the room and pulled Jodie to his side, bending to kiss her gently. "I have to go. Derek's on the job, and his brothers will be here within an hour or two. Nothing to worry about."

"Except you getting shot," Jodie replied worriedly.

He opened his jacket and showed her his gun.

"I know. You're indestructible. But come back in one piece, okay?" she asked softly.

He searched her eyes and smiled tenderly. "That's a deal. See you later." He winked at Margie and took one last look at Jodie before he left.

"How people change," Margie murmured dryly.

But Jodie wasn't really listening. Her eyes were still on Alexander's broad back as he went out the door.

Alexander and his group met somberly that evening to compare notes and plan strategy. They knew by now where Cara Dominguez was, who her cohorts were, and just how much Brody Vance knew about her operation. The security guard on the job at the Ritter warehouse was linked to the organization as well, but thought he was home free. What he didn't know was that Alexander had a court order to wiretap his office, and the agent overseeing that job had some interesting information to impart about a drug shipment that was still concealed in Ritter's warehouse. It was one that no one knew about until the wiretap. And it was a much bigger load than the one the drug unit had just busted.

The trick was going to be catching the thieves with the merchandise. It wasn't enough to know they were connected with it. They had to have hard evidence, facts that would stand up in court. They had to have a chain of evidence that would definitively link Cara to the drug shipment.

Just when Alexander thought he was ready to spring the trap, Cara Dominguez disappeared off the face of the earth. The security guard was immediately arrested, before he could flee, but he had nothing to say under advice of counsel.

When they went to the Ritter warehouse, with Colby Lane and Phillip Hunter, to appropriate the drug shipment, they found cartons of drilling equipment parts. Even with drug-sniffing dogs, they found no trace of the missing shipment. And everybody connected with Cara Dominguez suddenly developed amnesia and couldn't remember anything about her.

The only good thing about it was that the operation had obviously changed locations, and there was no further reason for anyone to target Jodie. Where it had moved was a job for the DEA to follow up on. Alexander was sure that Kennedy had something to do with the sudden disappearance of Cara, and the shipment, but he couldn't prove a thing. The only move he had left was to prosecute Kennedy for giving secret information to a known drug dealer, and that he could prove. He had Kennedy arraigned on charges of conspiracy to distribute controlled substances, which effectively removed the man from any chance of a future job in law enforcement — even if he managed to weasel out of a long jail term for what he'd already done.

Alexander returned to the Jacobsville ranch on Friday, to find Margie and Jodie in the kitchen making canapés while Cousin Derek and two other men sat at the kitchen table. Derek was sampling the sausage rolls while a taller dark-eyed man with jet-black hair oiled his handgun and a second dark-haired man with eyes as green as Alexander's sat glaring at his two companions.

"She's gone," Alexander said heavily. "Took a powder. We can't find a trace of her, so far, and the drug shipment vanished into thin air. Needless to say, I'm relieved on your behalf," he told a radiant Jodie. "But it's not what I wanted to happen."

"Your inside man slipped up," the green-eyed stranger said in a deep bass voice.

"I didn't have an inside man, Zeke," Alexander said, dropping into a chair with the other men. "More's the pity."

"Don't mind him," the other stranger said easily. "He's perfect. He never loses a case or misses a shot. And he can cook."

Zeke glared at him. "You could do with a few lessons in marksmanship, Josiah," he returned curtly. "You can't even hit a target."

"That's a fact," Derek agreed at once, dark eyes dancing. "He tried to shoot a snake once and took the mailbox down with a shotgun."

"I can hit what I aim at when I want to," Josiah said huffily. "I hated that damned mailbox. I shot it on purpose."

His brothers almost rolled on the floor laughing. Josiah sighed and poured himself another cup of coffee. "Then I guess I'm on a plane back to Oklahoma."

"And I'm on one to Wyoming." Zeke nodded.

Derek glared at them. "And I'm booked for a rodeo in Arizona. Listen, why don't we sell up and move down here? Texas has lots of ranches. In fact, I expect we could find one near here without a lot of trouble."

"You might at that," Alexander told them as he poured his own cup of coffee, taking the opportunity to ruffle Jodie's blond hair and smile tenderly down at her. "I hear the old Jacobs place is up for sale again. That eastern dude who took it over lost his shirt in the stock market. It's just as well. He didn't know much about horses anyway."

"It's a horse farm?" Josiah asked, interested.

Alexander nodded. "A seed herd of Arabians and a couple of foals they bred from racing stock. He had pipe dreams about entering a horse in the Kentucky Derby one day."

"Why'd he give it up?"

"Well, for one thing, he didn't know anything about horses. He wouldn't ask for advice from anybody who did, but he'd read this book. He figured he could do it himself. That was before he got kicked out of the barn the first time," he added in a droll tone.

Zeke made a rough sound. "I'm not keen on horses. And I work in Wyoming."

"You're a little too late, anyway," Margie interrupted, but she was watching Derek with new intensity. "We heard that one of Cash Grier's brothers came down here to look at it. Apparently, they're interested."

"Grier has brothers?" Jodie exclaimed. "What a horrifying thought! How many?"

"Three. They've been on the outs for a long time, but they're making overtures. It seems the ranch would get them close enough to Cash to try and heal the breach."

"That's one mean hombre," Derek ventured.

"He keeps the peace," Alexander defended him. "And he makes life interesting in town. Especially just lately."

"What's going on lately?" Derek wanted to know.

Alexander, Jodie and Margie exchanged secretive smiles. "Never mind," Alexander said. "There are other properties, if you're really interested. You might stop by one of the real estate agencies and stock up on brochures."

"He'll never leave Oklahoma," Derek said, nodding toward Josiah. "And Wyoming's the only place left that's sparsely populated enough to appeal to our family grizzly." He glanced at Margie and grinned. "However, I only need a temporary base of operations since I'm on the road so much. I might buy me a little cabin nearby and come serenade Margie on weekends when I'm in town."

Margie laughed, but she was flushed with excitement. "Might you, now?"

"Of course, you're set on a designing career," he mused.

"And you're hooked on breaking bones and spraining muscles in the rodeo circuit."

"We might find some common ground one day," Derek replied.

Margie only smiled. "Are you all staying for my Halloween party?" she asked the brothers.

Zeke finished his coffee and got up. "I don't do parties. Excuse me. I have to call the airline."

"I'm right behind you," Josiah said, following his brother with an apologetic smile.

"Well, I guess it's just me," Derek said. "What do you think, Marge, how about if I borrow one of Alex's suits and come as a college professor?"

She burst out laughing.

Alexander caught Jodie by the hand and pulled her out of the kitchen with him.

"Where are we going?" she asked.

"For a walk, now that nobody's shooting at us," he said, linking her fingers into his.

He led her out the front door and around to the side of the house, by the long fences that kept the cattle in.

"When do you have to go back to work?" he asked Jodie reluctantly.

"That wasn't exactly discussed," she confessed, with a secret smile, because he didn't know which job she was returning to take. "But I suppose next week will do nicely."

"I still think Brody Vance is involved in this somehow," he said flatly, turning to her. "I can't prove it yet, but I'm certain he's not as innocent as he's pretending to be."

"That's exactly what I think," she agreed, surprising him. "By the way," she added, "I quit my job before we came down here."

"You quit . . . good for you!" he exclaimed,

hugging her close. "I'm proud of you, Jodie!"

She laughed, holding on tight. "Don't be too proud. I'm still working for Mr. Ritter. But it's going to be in a totally different capacity."

"Doing what?" he asked flatly.

"I'm going to be working with Colby Lane as a computer security consultant," she told him.

"What about Hunter?" he asked.

"He's going back to Arizona with his wife. They're expecting a second child, and I think they want a little less excitement in their life right now," she confided with a grin. "So Colby Lane is taking over security. Mr. Ritter said I might have to do some traveling later on as a troubleshooter, but it wouldn't be often."

He was studying her with soft, quiet eyes. "As long as it's sporadic and not for too long, that's fine. You'll do well in security," he said. "Old man Ritter isn't as dense as I thought he was. I'm glad he's still keeping an eye on the company. Colby Lane will keep his security people on their toes just as well as Hunter did."

"I think Mr. Hunter is irritated that Cara managed to get into that warehouse parking lot," she ventured.

"He is. But it could have happened to anyone. Brody Vance is our wild card. He's going to need watching. And no, you can't offer to do it," he added firmly. "Let Lane set up his own surveillance. You stick to the job you're given and stop sticking your neck out."

"I like that!" she exclaimed. "And who was it who encouraged me to stick my neck out in the first place planting bugs near people in coffeehouses?"

He searched her eyes quietly. "You did a great job. I was proud of you. I always thought we might work well together."

"We did, didn't we?" she mused.

He pushed back wispy strands of loose hair from her cheek and studied her hungrily. "I have in mind another opportunity for mutual cooperation," he said, bending to her mouth.

ELEVEN

"What sort of mutual cooperation?" she whispered against his searching lips. "Does it involve guns and bugs?"

He smiled against her soft mouth. "I was thinking more of prophylactics . . ."

While Jodie was trying to let the extraordinary statement filter into her brain, and trying to decide whether to slug him or kiss him back, a loud voice penetrated their oblivion.

"Jodie!" Margie yelled. "Where are you?"

Alexander lifted his head. He seemed as dazed as she felt.

"Jodie!" Margie yelled more insistently.

"On my way!" Jodie yelled back.

"Sisters are a pain," he murmured on a long sigh.

She smiled at him. "I'm sure it's a minor disaster that only I can cope with," she assured him.

He chuckled. "Go ahead. But tonight," he

added in a deep, husky tone, "you're mine."

She flushed at the way he said it. She started to argue, but Margie was yelling again, so she ran toward the house instead.

Alexander stared hungrily at Jodie when she came down the stairs just before the first party guest arrived the next evening. They'd spent the day together, riding around the ranch and talking. There hadn't been any more physical encounters, but there was a new closeness between them that everyone noticed.

Jodie's blond hair was long and wavy. She was wearing a red dress with a long, ruffled hem, an elasticized neckline that was pushed off the shoulders, leaving her creamy skin visible. She was wearing high heels and more makeup than she usually put on. And she was breathtaking. He just shook his head, his eyes eating her as she came down the staircase, holding on to the banister.

"You could be dessert," he murmured when she reached him.

"So could you," she replied, adoring him with her eyes. "But you aren't even wearing a costume."

"I am so," he argued with a wry smile. "I'm disguised as a government agent."

"Alexander!" she wailed.

He chuckled and caught her fingers in his. "I look better than Derek does. He's coming as a rodeo cowboy, complete with banged-up chaps, worn-out boots, and a championship belt buckle the size of my foot."

"He'll look authentic," she replied.

He smiled. "So do I. Don't I?"

She sighed, loving the way he looked. "I suppose you do, at that. There's going to be a big crowd, Margie says."

He tilted her chin up to his eyes. "There won't be anyone here except the two of us, Jodie," he said quietly.

The way he was looking at her, she could almost believe it.

"I think Margie feels that way with Derek," she murmured absently. "Too bad his brothers wouldn't stay."

"They aren't the partying type," he said. "Neither are we, really."

She nodded. Her eyes searched his and she felt giddy all over at the shift in their relationship. It was as if all the arguments of years past were blown away like sand. She felt new, young, on top of the world. And if his expression was anything to go by, he felt the same way.

He traced her face with his eyes. "How do you feel about short engagements?" he asked out of the blue.

She was sure that it was a rhetorical question. "I suppose it depends on the people involved. If they knew each other well . . ."

"I've known you longer than any other woman in my life except my sister," he interrupted. His face tightened as he stared down at her with narrow, hungry eyes. "I want to marry you, Jodie."

She opened her mouth to speak and couldn't even manage words. The shock robbed her of speech.

He grimaced. "I thought it might come as a shock. You don't have to answer me this minute," he said easily, taking her hand. "You think about it for a while. Let's go mingle with the guests as they come in and spend the night dancing. Then I'll ask you again."

She went along with him unprotesting, but she was certain she was hearing things. Alexander wasn't a marrying man. He must be temporarily out of his mind with worry over his unsolved case. But he didn't look like the product of a deranged mind, and the way he held Jodie's hand tight in his, and the way he watched her, were convincing.

Not only that, but he had eyes for her alone. Kirry didn't come, but there were plenty of other attractive women at the party. None of them attracted so much as a glance from Alexander. He danced only with Jodie, and held her so closely that people who knew both of them started to speculate openly on their changed relationship.

"People are watching us," Jodie murmured as they finished one dance only to start right into another one.

"Let them watch," he said huskily. His eyes fell to her soft mouth. "I'm glad you work in Houston, Jodie. I won't have to find excuses to commute to Jacobsville to see you."

"You never liked me before," she murmured out loud.

"I never got this close to you before," he countered. "I've lived my whole life trying to forget the way my mother was, Jodie," he confessed. "She gave me emotional scars that I still carry. I kept women at a safe distance. I actually thought I had you at a safe distance, too," he added on a chuckle. "And then I started taking you around for business reasons and got caught in my own web."

"Did you, really?" she murmured with wonder.

"Careful," he whispered. "I'm dead serious." He bent and brushed his mouth beside hers, nuzzling her cheek with his nose. "It's too late to go back, Jodie. I can't let go."

His arm contracted. She gasped softly at the increased intimacy of the contact. She could feel the hunger in him. Her own body began to vibrate faintly as she realized how susceptible she was.

"You be careful," she countered breathlessly. "I'm on fire! You could find yourself on the floor in a closet, being ravished, if you keep this up."

"If that's a promise, lead me to a closet," he said, only half joking.

She laughed. He didn't.

In fact, his arm contracted even more and he groaned softly at her ear. "Jodie," he said in a choked tone, "how do you feel about runaway marriages?"

"Excuse me?"

He lifted his head and looked down into her eyes with dark intensity. "Runaway marriage. You get in a car, run away to Mexico in the middle of somebody's Halloween party and get married." His arm brought her closer. "They're binding even in this country. We could get to the airport in about six minutes, and onto a plane in less than an hour."

"To where?" she burst out, aghast.

"Anywhere in Mexico," he groaned, his eyes biting into hers as he lifted his head. "We can be married again in Jacobsville whenever you like."

"Then why go to Mexico tonight?" she asked, flustered.

His hand slid low on her spine and pulled her hips into his with a look that made her blush.

"That is not a good reason to go to Mexico on the spur of the moment," she said, while her body told her brain to shut up.

"That's what you think." His expression was eloquent.

"But what if I said yes?" she burst out. "You could end up tied to me for life, when all you want is immediate relief! And speaking of relief, there's a bedroom right up the stairs . . . !"

He stopped dancing. His face was solemn. "Tell me you wouldn't mind a quick fling in my bed, Jodie," he challenged. "Tell me your conscience wouldn't bother you at all."

She sighed. "I'd like to," she began.

"But your parents didn't raise you that way," he concluded for her. "In fact, my father was like that," he added quietly. "He was old-fashioned and I'm like him. There haven't even been that many women, if you'd like to know, Jodie," he confessed. "And right now, I wish there hadn't been even one."

"That is the sweetest thing to say," she whispered, and pulled his face down so that she could kiss him.

"As it happens, I mean it." He kissed her back, very lightly. "Run away with me," he challenged. "Right now!"

It was crazy. He had to be out of his mind. But the temptation to get him to a minister before he changed his mind was all-consuming. She was suddenly caught up in the same excitement she saw in his face. "But you're so conventional!"

"I'll be very conventional again first thing tomorrow," he promised. "Tonight, I'm going for broke. Grab a coat. Don't tell anybody where we're going. I'll think up something to say to Margie."

She glanced toward the back of the room, where Margie was watching them excitedly and whispering something to Derek that made him laugh.

"All right. We're both crazy, but I'm not arguing with you. Tell her whatever you like. Make it good," she told him, and dashed up the staircase.

He was waiting for her at the front door. He looked irritated.

"What's wrong?" Jodie asked when she reached him. Her heart plummeted. "Changed your mind?"

"Not on your life!" He caught her arm and pulled her out the door, closing it quickly behind them. "Margie's too smart for her own good. Or Derek is."

"You can't put anything past Margie," she said, laughing with relief as they ran down the steps and toward the garage, where he kept his Jaguar.

"Or Derek," he murmured, chuckling.

He unlocked the door with his keyless entry and popped out the laser key with his thumb on the button. He looked down at her hesitantly. "I'm game if you are," he told her. "But you can still back out if you want to."

She shook her head, her eyes full of dreams. "You might never be in the mood again."

"That's a laugh." He put her inside and minutes later, they were en route to the airport.

Holding hands all the way during the

flight, making plans, they arrived in El Paso with bated breath. Alexander rented a car at the airport and they drove across the border, stopping at customs and looking so radiant that the guard guessed their purpose immediately.

"You're going over to get married, I'd bet," the man said with a huge grin. *"Buena suerte,"* he added, handing back their identification. "And drive carefully!"

"You bet!" Alexander told him as he drove off.

They found a small chapel and a minister willing to perform the ceremony after a short conversation with a police officer near a traffic light.

Jodie borrowed a peso from the minister's wife for luck and was handed a small bouquet of silk flowers to hold while the words were spoken, in Spanish, that would make them man and wife.

Alexander translated for her, his eyes soft and warm and possessive as the minister pronounced them man and wife at last. He drew a ring out of his pocket, a beautiful embossed gold band, which he slid onto her finger. It was a perfect fit. She recognized it as one she'd sighed over years ago in a jewelry shop she'd gone to with Margie when they were dreaming about marriage in the distant future. She'd been back to the shop over the years to make sure it was still there. Apparently Margie had told Alexander about it.

They signed the necessary documents, Alexander paid the minister, and they got back into the car with a marriage license.

Jodie stared at her ring and her new husband with wide-eyed wonder. "We must be crazy," she commented.

He laughed. "We're not crazy. We're very sensible. First we have an elopement, then we have a honeymoon, then we have a normal wedding with Margie and our friends." He glanced at her with twinkling eyes. "You said you didn't have to be back at work until next week. We'll have our honeymoon before you go back."

"Where, exactly, did you have in mind for a honeymoon?" she asked.

Three hours later, tangled with Alexander in a big king-size bed with waves pounding the shore outside the window, she lay in the shadows of the moonlit Gulf of Mexico. The hotel was first class, the food was supposed to be the best in Galveston, the beach was like sugar sand. But all she saw was Alexander's face above hers as her body throbbed in the molasses slow rhythm of his kisses on her breasts on cool, crisp sheets.

"You taste like candy," he whispered against her belly.

"You never said I was sweet before," she teased breathlessly.

"You always were. I didn't know how to say it. You gave me the shakes every time I got near you." His mouth opened on her diaphragm and pressed down, hard.

She gasped at the warm pleasure of it. Her hands tangled in his thick, dark hair. "That was mutual, too." She drew his face to her breasts and coaxed his mouth onto them. "This is very nice," she murmured unsteadily.

"It gets better." His hands found her in a new and invasive way. She started to protest, only to find his mouth crushing down over her parted lips about the same time that his movements lifted her completely off the bed in a throbbing wave of unexpected pleasure.

"Oh, you like that, do you?" he murmured against her mouth. "How about this . . . ?"

She cried out. His lips stifled the sound and his leg moved between both of hers. He kissed her passionately while his lean hips shifted and she felt him in an intimacy they hadn't yet shared.

He felt her body jerk as she tried to reject

the shock of invasion, but his mouth gentled hers, his hands soothed her, teased her, coaxed her into allowing the slow merging of their bodies.

She gasped, her hands biting into his back in mingled fear and excitement.

"It won't hurt long," he whispered reassuringly, and his tongue probed her lips as he began a slow, steady rhythm that rippled down her nerves like pure joy on a roller coaster of pleasure.

"That's it," he murmured against her eager lips. "Come up against me and find the pressure and the rhythm that you need. That's it. That's . . . it!"

She was amazed that he didn't mind letting her experiment, that he was willing to help her experience him. She'd heard some horror stories about wedding nights from former friends. This wasn't one. She'd found a man who wanted eager participation, not passive acceptance. She moved and shifted and he laughed roughly, his deep voice throbbing with pleasure, as her seeking body kindled waves of delight in his own.

She was on fire with power. She moved under him, invited him, challenged him, provoked him. And he went with her, every step of the way up the ladder to a mutual climax that groaned out at her ear in ripples of satiation. She clung to him, shivering in the explosive aftermath of an experience that exceeded her wildest hopes.

"And now you know," he whispered, kissing her eyelids closed.

"Now I know." She nose-dived into his damp throat and clung while they slowly settled back to earth again.

"I love you, baby," he whispered tenderly.

Joy flooded through her. "I love you, too!" she whispered breathlessly.

He curled her into his body with a long yawn and with the ocean purring like a wet kitten outside the windows, they drifted off into a warm, soft sleep.

"Hey."

She heard his voice at her ear. Then there was an aroma, a delicious smell of fresh coffee, rich and dark and delicious.

Her eyes didn't even open, but her head followed the retreat of the coffee.

"I thought that would do it. Breakfast," Alexander coaxed. "We've got your favorite, pecan waffles with bacon."

Her eyes opened. "You remembered!"

He grinned at her. "I know what you like." His lips pursed. "Especially after last night."

She laughed, dragging herself out of bed

in the slip she'd worn to bed, because it was still too soon to sleep in nothing at all. She was shy with him.

He was completely dressed, right down to his shoes. He gave her an appreciative sweep of his green eyes that took in her bare feet and her disheveled hair.

"You look wonderful like that," he said. "I always knew you would."

"When was that, exactly?" she chided, taking a seat at the table facing the window. "Before or after you accused me of being a layabout?"

"Ouch!" he groaned.

"It's okay. I forgive you," she said with a wicked glance. "I could never hold a grudge against a man who was that good in bed."

"And just think, I was very subdued last night, in deference to your first time."

She gasped. "Well!"

His eyebrows arched. "Think of the possibilities. If you aren't too delicate after last night, we could explore some of them later."

"Later?"

"I had in mind taking you around town and showing you off," he said, flipping open a napkin. "They have all sorts of interesting things to see here."

She sipped coffee, trying to ignore her body, which was making emphatic statements about what *it* wanted to do with the day.

He was watching her with covert, wise eyes. "On the other hand," he murmured as he nibbled a pancake, "if you were feeling lazy, we could just lie around in the bed and listen to the ocean, while we . . ."

Her hand poised over the waffle. "While we . . . ?"

He began to smile. She laughed. The intimacy was new and secret, and exciting. She rushed through the waffle and part of the bacon, and then pushed herself away from the table and literally threw herself into his arms across the chair. He prided himself on his control, because they actually almost made it to the bed. . . .

Two days later, worn-out, and not because of any sightseeing trip, they dragged themselves into the ranch house with a bag full of peace offerings for Margie which included seashells, baskets, a pretty ruffled sundress and some taffy.

Margie gave them a long, amused look. "There is going to have to be a wedding here," she informed them. "It won't do to run off to Mexico and get married, you have to do it in Jacobsville before anybody will believe you're really man and wife."

"I don't mind," Alexander said complacently, "but I'm not making the arrangements."

"Jodie and I can do that."

"But I have to go back to work," she told Margie, and went forward to hand her the bag and hug her. "And I haven't even told you about my new job!"

"What about your new husband?" Alexander groaned. "Are you going to desert me?"

She gave him a wicked glance. "Don't you have to talk to somebody about ranch business? Margie doesn't even know that I'm changing jobs!"

He sighed. "That's all husbands are good for," he murmured to himself. "You marry a woman, and she runs off and leaves you to gossip with a girlfriend."

"My sister-in-law, if you please," Jodie corrected him with a grin. "I'll cook you a nice apple pie for later, Alexander," she promised.

"Okay, I do take bribes," he had to confess. He grinned at her. "But now that we're married, couldn't you find something else to call me? Something a little less formal?"

She thought about it for a minute. "Darling," she said.

He looked at her with an odd expression,

smiled as if he couldn't help himself, and made a noise like a tiger. He went out the back door while they were still laughing.

Jodie moved into her new job with a little apprehension, because of what she'd said to Brody Vance, but he was as genial as if no cross words had ever been spoken between them. Cara Dominguez still hadn't been heard from or seen, neither had her accomplice. There was still a shipment of drugs missing, that had to be in the warehouse somewhere, but guards and stepped up surveillance assured that the drug dealers couldn't get near the warehouse to search for it.

One of Cara's rivals in the business was arrested in a guns-for-drugs deal in Houston that made national and international headlines. Alexander told Jodie about it just before the wire services broke the story, and assured her that Cara's organization was going to be next on the list of objectives for his department.

Meanwhile, Jodie learned the ropes of computer security and went back to school to finish her certification, with Alexander's blessing. Margie came up to see her while she was arranging a showing of her new designs with a local modeling agency and a department store that Kirry didn't work for.

Alexander kept shorter hours and did more delegating of chores, so that he could be at home when Jodie was. They bought a small house on the outskirts of Houston. Margie arranged to help Jodie with the decorating scheme. She was still amazed at the change in her best friend, who was now independent, strong-willed, hardworking and nobody's doormat.

There was still the retro coffeehouse, of course, and one night Jodie had a phone call from the owner, Johnny. She listened, exploded with delight, and ran to tell Alexander the news.

"The publisher wants to buy my poems!" she exclaimed. "He wants to include them in an anthology of Texas poetry! Isn't it exciting?"

"It's exciting," he agreed, bending to kiss her warmly. "Now tell the truth. They're about me, aren't they?"

She sighed. "Yes, they're about you. But I'm afraid this will be the only volume of poetry I ever create."

"Really? Why?"

She nibbled his chin. "Because misery is what makes good poetry. And just between us two," she added as her fingers went to his shirt buttons, "I'm far too happy to write good poetry ever again."

He guided her fingers down his shirt, smiling secretively. "I have plans to keep you that way, too," he murmured deeply.

And he did.

ABOUT THE AUTHOR

The prolific author of over one hundred books, **Diana Palmer** got her start as a newspaper reporter. A multi-*New York Times* bestselling author and one of the top ten romance writers in America, she has a gift for telling the most sensual tales with charm and humor. Diana lives with her family in Cornelia, Georgia.

We hope you have enjoyed this Large Print book. Other Thorndike, Wheeler, and Chivers Press Large Print books are available at your library or directly from the publishers.

For information about current and upcoming titles, please call or write, without obligation, to:

Publisher
Thorndike Press
295 Kennedy Memorial Drive
Waterville, ME 04901
Tel. (800) 223-1244

or visit our Web site at:

www.gale.com/thorndike
www.gale.com/wheeler

OR

Chivers Large Print
published by BBC Audiobooks Ltd
St James House, The Square
Lower Bristol Road
Bath BA2 3SB
England
Tel. +44(0) 800 136919
email: bbcaudiobooks@bbc.co.uk
www.bbcaudiobooks.co.uk

All our Large Print titles are designed for easy reading, and all our books are made to last.